"I Can't Believe This Is Happening," Tara Whispered, Her Eyes Wide. "It's Three O'clock In The Morning, And A Half-Naked Prince Has Just Suggested I Become Engaged To Him."

"Would it help if I were dressed differently?" Nicholas murmured with a smile.

"It would help if you left," she answered.

Nicholas touched the soft underside of her chin and tilted her head upward. She looked so distressed and lost that an odd tenderness slid through him. He wanted to soothe away the confusion and discomfort he read on her face. It was a strange, overwhelming need that ate at him.

"This…*arrangement* is going to work out very well," he assured her, rubbing his thumb over her silky bottom lip. He felt a sudden lick of arousal curl deep in his stomach. "In fact, it could be perfect…." And then he took her mouth with his.

Each member of this royal family finds the love of a commoner to be most uncommon of all!

Dear Reader,

Looking for romances with a healthy dose of passion? Don't miss Silhouette Desire's red-hot May lineup of passionate, powerful and provocative love stories!

Start with our MAN OF THE MONTH, *His Majesty, M.D.,* by bestselling author Leanne Banks. This latest title in the ROYAL DUMONTS miniseries features an explosive engagement of convenience between a reluctant royal and a determined heiress. Then, in Kate Little's *Plain Jane & Doctor Dad,* the new installment of Desire's continuity series DYNASTIES: THE CONNELLYS, a rugged Connelly sweeps a pregnant heroine off her feet.

A brooding cowboy learns about love and family in *Taming Blackhawk,* a SECRETS! title by Barbara McCauley. Reader favorite Sara Orwig offers a brand-new title in the exciting TEXAS CATTLEMAN'S CLUB: THE LAST BACHELOR series. In *The Playboy Meets His Match,* enemies become lovers and then some.

A sexy single mom is partnered with a lonesome rancher in Kathie DeNosky's *Cassie's Cowboy Daddy.* And in Anne Marie Winston's *Billionaire Bachelors: Garrett,* sparks fly when a tycoon shares a cabin with the woman he believes was his stepfather's mistress.

Bring passion into your life this month by indulging in all six of these sensual sizzlers.

Enjoy!

Joan Marlow Golan

Joan Marlow Golan
Senior Editor, Silhouette Desire

Please address questions and book requests to:
Silhouette Reader Service
U.S.: 3010 Walden Ave., P.O. Box 1325, Buffalo, NY 14269
Canadian: P.O. Box 609, Fort Erie, Ont. L2A 5X3

His Majesty, M.D.
LEANNE BANKS

Published by Silhouette Books
America's Publisher of Contemporary Romance

This book is dedicated to all the people
who volunteered during and after the crisis of 9/11.
You define the true meaning of heroism.

 SILHOUETTE BOOKS

ISBN 0-373-76435-9

HIS MAJESTY, M.D.

Copyright © 2002 by Leanne Banks

This edition published by arrangement with Harlequin Books S.A.

Visit Silhouette at www.eHarlequin.com

Printed in U.S.A.

LEANNE BANKS,

a bestselling author of romance, lives in her native Virginia with her husband, son and daughter. Recognized for both her sensual and humorous writing with two Career Achievement Awards from *Romantic Times,* Leanne likes creating a story with a few grins, a generous kick of sensuality and characters that hang around after the book is finished. Leanne believes romance readers are the best readers in the world because they understand that love is the greatest miracle of all. You can contact Leanne online at leannebbb@aol.com or write to her at P.O. Box 1442, Midlothian, VA 23113. A SASE for a reply would be greatly appreciated.

Prologue

"**I** want you to be nice to this one," Queen Anna Catherine said with an imperious tone that Nicholas believed had been genetically implanted. "This one has great potential."

He smothered a yawn as he joined his mother for tea in her favorite parlor in the palace. They all had great potential. His mother had been trying to find a wife for him since he'd slept in a cradle. She hadn't succeeded yet, and if he had anything to do with it, she never would. He would marry if and when and whom he damn well pleased.

"I'm serious, Nicholas. No shenanigans this time," she said with a warning glint in her eyes. "She could be important to Marceau."

Nicholas's gut knotted. Uh-oh. She was going to

pull the good of the country routine again. "How important?" he asked skeptically.

"Her father is Grant York. He's known as a business genius. He owns a conglomerate of luxury resorts all over the world."

Nicholas nodded with little enthusiasm. "Tourists," he said.

"Yes," his mother said, as if she too had struggled with the idea of their island country being invaded by hordes of outsiders. "A connection with York Enterprises would provide a boon for our economy. It's not in the best interest of our citizens to keep Marceau a secret."

"You know I'm not interested in getting married," he told her, hating the sharp poke of responsibility he felt.

"You don't have to marry Tara York. I just want you to be a kind escort during her stay here at the palace," his mother said. "However, it wouldn't hurt you to settle down."

"Yes, it would," Nicholas said, feeling a noose tighten around his neck. "I think what you meant to say is that it wouldn't hurt *you* if I settled down."

Queen Anna Catherine sighed. "You are undoubtedly the most blunt of your brothers."

Nicholas thought of his brothers and couldn't disagree. "It could be worse. Michel will rule. He needs to know how to be tactful in order to deal with the royal advisors. On the flip side, you get to refer to me as 'my son, the doctor,'" he said, with a sly grin because his mother had been against him going for his medical degree. His brother Michel's negotiation skills had smoothed the way, and for that, Nicholas would always be grateful. And for facilitating his medical career, he would also be indebted to both his brother *and* his mother.

Queen Anna's eyes lit with grudging admiration. "You've chosen a difficult path. To be a royal and a medical doctor will never be easy."

"But nothing else will do," he said and felt the truth echo in his bones. By luck he had been born a prince, but Nicholas knew his destiny had always been medicine. "Medicine is as demanding as a wife."

His mother raised his eyebrows. "Many men have both," she said. "But we can save that discussion for another day. Tara York will arrive tomorrow. Show her a good time for the sake of Marceau."

Nicholas rolled his eyes at his mother's melodramatic request, but nodded. "Always for the sake of country," he muttered, rising. He gave a brief bow of his head in respect, then headed for the door.

"A shave and a haircut wouldn't hurt, Nicholas," Queen Anna suggested.

Nicholas paused. His mother was nothing if not shrewd. She knew he'd deliberately discouraged more than a few of her matchmaking attempts by sporting shaggy hair and three-day stubble. Seeing the weariness on his mother's face, Nicholas bit back a retort. Although she had tried to hide it, the search for conclusive information on his long-lost brother was clearly wearing on her. His mother had seemed to age years during the last few months. She looked almost vulnerable. The knowledge grabbed at his gut, because Queen Anna Catherine had hitherto been known as The Iron Lady. "For the sake of Marceau," he said wryly, running his hand over his stubbled chin.

One

"**I** think you've just been out-geeked," Nicholas's sister, Michelina, whispered in his ear as Tara York stumbled into the palace's grand entrance hall.

Nicholas blinked at the sight that beheld him. Tara York's brown hair was pulled back into an unbecoming bun, Coke-bottle lenses covered her eyes, and she wore a matronly dress he would expect to see on a woman twice her age.

"Quick," Michelina continued, sotto voce. "Let me call Fashion Emergency."

Although he couldn't disagree, Nicholas felt a ripple of irritation. "Not everyone feels compelled to look like an advertisement for *Vogue Paris* when they walk out the door. You may find it difficult to believe, but there are more important things in the world than choosing between Dior and Versace.''

''Perhaps I might have the opportunity to experience some of those choices if Mother wouldn't keep me trapped in the palace like Rapunzel,'' Michelina retorted. ''Either way, I think I can safely say that Miss York didn't choose that dress from Dior or Versace. You must admit, Mother has never sent you a prospect like this.''

''She's not a prospect. She's a guest,'' Nicholas said, and moved toward Tara as she stumbled again.

''Excuse me, Your Highness,'' Tara said, and gave a quick dutiful curtsey. ''I'm afraid the long flight has upset my equilibrium.''

He automatically reached out a hand to steady her, but she pulled back. ''I'm fine, thank you,'' she murmured.

''Miss York,'' Nicholas began.

''Please call me Tara,'' she said with a slight, tight smile that Nicholas thought he might like if it were just a bit wider and more sincere. She waved her hand to encompass Michelina. ''And you must also be Your Highness.''

His lips twitched. ''Not necessary. I'm Nicholas, and this is my sister, Michelina.''

Michelina dutifully stepped forward. ''We're so pleased you could visit our country, Tara. You must tell me if there is anything I can do to make your stay more comfortable.''

Tara adjusted her thick glasses. ''Thank you, Michelina. I need to make sure there's an Internet connection in my room."

Michelina hesitated in surprise. "An Internet connection?"

Nicholas watched a sliver of concern cross Tara's face. "Yes, it's actually the only thing I require. You do have phone lines in the palace, don't you?"

Michelina nodded. "Oh, of course we do. It's just that most of our visitors prefer to enjoy outdoor activities, especially our beautiful beaches."

Tara shrugged. "I'm sure they're beautiful, but I burn so easily," she confided, adjusting her glasses on her nose again. "I'll be able to keep busy inside, thank you."

Michelina gave a slow nod of wonder. "As you wish, but if you should change your mind, please feel free to let Nicholas or me know."

Baffled by the strange creature standing before him, Nicholas studied her. The thick glasses couldn't hide the intelligence in her eyes. Her courteous tone couldn't hide the fact that she didn't want to be here. "I'll have your bags taken to your room. Would you like a snack before you freshen up? There will be a small dinner party held in your honor this evening."

"A dinner party in my honor?" Tara echoed in dismay. In fact, Nicholas might call it dread. He knew all about the emotion because he felt exactly the same way about most of the formal palace parties. "That's not necessary," she said, a shade desperately.

Nicholas felt a twinge of sympathy for the woman. "My mother, the queen, insists," he said.

Realization crossed her face, and she nodded with a sigh. She met his gaze and, despite her thick lenses, in that one moment, Nicholas felt an inexplicable understanding pass between them.

Tara averted her gaze. "If it's not too much trouble, I would appreciate some juice. And I'm sure a shower will do wonders. Thank you for your hospitality."

"Our pleasure," Nicholas said, curious despite himself. He introduced Tara to a palace aide and watched her walk down the hallway. He wasn't sure he'd seen a more hideous dress, but the ugly garment didn't conceal Tara's shapely calves. His curiosity was piqued.

His sister squeezed his shoulder. "You have my sympathy this time. Mother can't possibly be serious about a match with that woman."

"It doesn't matter if Mother is serious about her matchmaking attempts. I'm not," he said.

"But an Internet junkie. How in the world will you entertain her?"

Nicholas loved his sister, but he also knew Michelina tended to jump to conclusions. "Something tells me there's more here than what meets the eye," he said, and decided if he was going to be assigned the task of entertaining Tara York, he might as well satisfy his curiosity about her.

Tara ditched her glasses the second she entered her suite. Pacing the length of the large, elegant bedroom furnished with 18th-century antiques, she massaged her temples and sighed. She didn't need glasses, and they actually gave her a headache. The heavy lenses, however, had served—and would continue to serve—an important purpose. They, along with her dumpy clothing and her deliberate social ineptitude, kept the dogs after her father's fortune at bay.

Tara suspected Prince Nicholas might not appreciate being called a dog, and he was certainly better looking than a dog, but in her mind, all marital prospects presented by her father were dogs.

They all wanted her because of what her father could do for them, and no matter how much Tara argued with him, her father insisted marriage was in her best interest for his peace of mind and her own safety.

She bent down to toss her shoes into the closet, turned her head to the side and the room suddenly tilted. Struggling to steady herself, she stubbed her toe on the edge of the carpet and pitched forward. Swearing under her breath, she felt the sting of panic that came from being out of control. Standing perfectly still, she took a deep breath to calm herself.

Her clumsiness had been the bane of her existence. Ever since she'd been a child, Tara had fought a propensity for tripping over her own feet. It was one of those things that seemed to come and go with no advance notice. After a broken arm and a fractured ankle, her father had become overprotective. He always referred to it as her "little problem." Tara understood part of his uneasiness about her clumsiness.

She agreed it was best for her not to get behind the

wheel of an automobile, and she didn't attempt dancing for fear of injuring someone. She shuddered to think of the injury suits people would file against her and her father. She agreed that she was certainly more clumsy than the average person, but she did not agree that a husband was the answer to her "little problem."

More than anything, Tara craved a feeling of accomplishment and independence. She wanted to contribute. She didn't want to be that giant sucking sound her father heard just before he fell asleep at night. She had often feared she was a disappointment to her father—certainly a liability—and she wanted to prove herself, not just to him, but to herself as well.

Taking careful steps, she unpacked her laptop computer and carried it to the desk. After placing it on the desktop, she stroked the machine. Inside that computer lay the secrets to her progress and the promise of her future. So far, she'd earned two college degrees over the Internet, and she was currently working on her master's degree.

Nicholas Dumont's curious gaze flitted through her mind. Although he was handsome and she had to admire the fact that he'd earned his degree in medicine, Tara knew his family must want something from her father. On the other hand, her father probably loved the idea of the built-in security level that royals provided. He was no doubt quite prepared to give the Dumonts something they wanted if they gave him something he wanted—a husband for his daughter.

A bitter taste filled Tara's mouth. She didn't want

a husband, royal or otherwise. She glanced at the array of ugly dresses the palace aide had hung for her in the closet, then back at her computer. She wanted freedom, and she knew how to get it. She also knew how to be the opposite of alluring and seductive.

Nicholas was probably more intelligent than most of the men she sent packing, but he was still a man, and no man in his right mind would want her, with her thick glasses, lack of style and "little problem." Tara knew she was completely resistible.

After sitting through five courses and politely answering more than a dozen questions about her father while she evaded questions about herself, Tara wished she could disappear. The calories from the chocolate mousse alone, she reminded herself dryly, would ensure she wouldn't be disappearing any time soon. She glanced around the table and concluded that with the exception of royal blood and position, the Dumonts were like most families—a combination of functional and dysfunctional.

Throughout the meal, she felt Nicholas's curious gaze on her, but tried to ignore him. She hadn't been at all successful. She couldn't help noticing his hands as he cut the beef burgundy and lifted the glass of red wine to his mouth. They were strong and masculine, but something made her think they were also gentle. When his mother complimented him, she heard his muffled long-suffering sigh. She wondered how appalled he was at the thought of being paired with her and hid her smile of amusement behind her wineglass.

She sensed Queen Anna's offspring viewed their mother with a mixture of emotions; love and protectiveness interspersed with impatience at her attempts to orchestrate their lives. Michelina was quiet and appeared to be brooding. The heir, Michel, seemed to bite his tongue more than once. His American wife, Maggie, divided her attention between distracting Michel from his annoyance, talking to Michel's son, Max and trying to put Tara at ease. The love between the three of them was palpable.

True love mystified her. Her parents had not been in love, and she'd rarely had an opportunity to observe the real thing. Tara felt a tiny dart of longing as she watched them, but she refused to examine the emotion too closely. Marriage was not for her. She didn't want to transfer her dependence from one man to another.

"We're all quite proud of Nicholas," Queen Anna said to Tara. "He graduated at the top of his class."

"Pushing, pushing," Nicholas muttered under his breath, and took a sip of wine.

"And he's an excellent swordsman," Queen Anna continued. "I'm sure he's too modest to tell you he has represented Marceau and won many competitions. It's all Nicholas can do to dodge the magazines featuring royal bachelors. He's always a favorite."

"Stick a fork in me. I'm done," he muttered, then cleared his throat. "Mother," he said. "After Ms. York's long flight, I'm sure she would enjoy some fresh air." He turned his gaze toward Tara. "May I show you the balcony?"

Escape! Tara's heart raced with the anticipation of leaving the endless dinner. "Yes. I'd like that very much, thank you," she said, and quickly stood, nearly knocking her chair to the floor in her haste.

Nicholas grabbed the chair and righted it, then stood and offered his arm. "Excuse us," he said, and led her from the room.

As soon as they rounded the corner to the balcony, Tara removed her hand from his arm. She felt a shiver of relief when he stepped away at the same time she did. He clearly was not attracted to her.

She moved to the railing and inhaled the sweetly scented air. A combination of moonlight and strategically placed floodlights illuminated the beautiful gardens below. No matter what city she'd visited during her father's mandatory find-a-groom tour during the last six months, Tara had been too busy with her studies to enjoy the moonlight. The greenery and blooming flowers had a soothing effect on her.

"You'll have to forgive my mother. Subtlety isn't her strong suit," Nicholas said in a deep confiding tone.

Tara turned and allowed herself a moment to study him. Tall with broad shoulders, he gazed down at her with an inviting glint in his light blue eyes. One side of his lips cocked upward in a half grin. Dressed in a dark suit, he wore the clothing with masculine carelessness. She suspected he would be much happier with his sleeves pushed up his arms. Nicholas emanated an intellectual toughness combined with a social ease that drew her. He wasn't pushy or predatory like some of the other men her father had urged her toward. In another situation, she might even find him appealing.

She tensed at the thought and mentally slammed on the brakes. "It's nice that your mother is proud of you, and it sounds as if your accomplishments warrant her pride. I think everyone wants that feeling of accomplishment."

He lifted a dark eyebrow and nodded. "And you?"

"Of course," she said automatically.

"What would you like to accomplish?" he probed.

Tara's throat tightened at the question though, she knew he was sincere. At least, he appeared sincere. But she hadn't revealed her personal goals to anyone, she didn't want others making fun of her. By the kindness in Nicholas's eyes, she suspected he wouldn't make fun. Still, she thought it would be easier to disclose her bra size than her personal dreams, and she was pretty sure he wasn't interested in her bra size.

"My goals are currently under construction," she said.

He nodded. "Fair enough. Mine are too, but your answer tells me nothing about you. It's my job to entertain you, and I can't do that unless I know what's important to you. Or at least what you like and don't like."

"No, you don't," she said, looking away from him and inhaling a draft of vanilla-scented air. She felt him move closer, and an odd frisson of awareness shimmied down her nerve endings.

"No, I don't what?"

"You don't need to entertain me," she said, forcing herself to meet his gaze dead-on. "I can entertain myself."

He blinked in surprise, then cocked his head to one side. "What if I *want* to entertain you?"

"I can't imagine why. I don't think we have much in common," she said, even though a part of her wondered.

"We don't know what we have in common unless we get to know each other."

True, but Tara knew everything she needed to know. Her father wanted her to marry this man, and she didn't want to marry anyone. She struggled with the desire to rip away the polite social veneer covering the awkward situation. She wanted to say *I don't want to marry you, you don't want to marry me—so let's bag the pretense.*

"I appreciate your hospitality, but I'm quite an introvert, so I'll be perfectly content to spend time alone in my room and explore the palace and its grounds…by myself. Please feel free to carry on with your regular schedule."

Tick-tock, tick-tock. Her thesis was calling her, and she needed to rest to get over her jet lag. She wondered how she was going to maintain her schedule on her thesis without becoming a total recluse during her stay in Marceau.

"There must be something we can offer you," Nicholas said. "Do you ride horses?"

With her lack of coordination? she thought wryly. "I'm sorry. No."

"Speed boat?"

Tara had learned long ago that putting herself behind the controls of anything with an engine was a prescription for disaster. She shook her head.

"Bicycle riding?"

"No, thank you. What can I say? I lead a quiet, boring life." *I promise I would bore you to tears,* she wanted to say. "Speaking of quiet, I think jet lag is kicking in. You wouldn't mind if I retire to my room, would you?"

Frowning, he shook his head. "No. I'll walk you to your room."

Tara wanted to tell him it wasn't necessary, but bit her tongue. She didn't need to be a shrew—she just needed to be firm. "Thank you." He escorted her down three long hallways, and although they didn't talk, Tara felt hypersensitive in his presence. When she glimpsed her room, a rush of relief raced through her.

"Thank you again for your hospitality," she said, grasping the doorknob as if it were a lifeline. If she hurried, she wouldn't have to meet Nicholas's unsettling curious gaze again.

He stopped her with a hand on her shoulder. He took her hand, and stopped her breath and heart at the same time. She watched in amazement as he lifted her hand and brushed his lips over it. "Welcome to Marceau, Tara," he said. "If there is anything you need, call me."

A hot, sensual thought stole across her mind. Nicholas gave the impression he could take care of all of a woman's needs. Needs she'd decided to put off for at least the next decade, she reminded herself. She swallowed. "I can't think of a thing at the moment." *Truer words were never spoken,* she thought, chiding herself for her muddled mental state. "But thank you," she managed, and removed her hand from his. "Good night."

"A bientôt, chérie."

Biting her lip, Tara entered her room and closed the door and Nicholas Dumont behind her. If she weren't careful, she could like him, and that wouldn't be a good idea at all.

Nicholas glanced at the clock on his nightstand and swore. 3:00 a.m. He threw back the sheets and headed for the small refrigerator in the parlor of his suite. He usually slept like the dead.

There was no good reason for his insomnia except perhaps his distraction with his brother Jacques, who had been missing for over twenty years. The family had only recently learned that Jacques might be alive. A team of investigators had been hired to scour the globe for Jacques, but every once in a while Nicholas wondered what had become of his youngest brother after the accident.

Nicholas rolled his shoulders as he glanced inside the small refrigerator. Beer, but no water. He frowned and shrugged, deciding to go down to the kitchen and grab a bottle. It wasn't as if he had anything else to do. He pulled on a pair of shorts and walked out of his suite.

Another thing that weighed heavily on his mind was that he was trying to find a way to make his medical training of use to the people of Marceau. His oldest brother, Michel, the heir apparent, made no secret of his wish for Nicholas to become official medical consulate, but Nicholas himself craved a more direct, healing role.

Finally, there was Tara York, he thought as he glanced down the hallway to the room where she slept. The woman wasn't at all what he'd expected, and she seemed to be doing her level best to discourage his attention. He should be whooping with joy that he wouldn't be forced to entertain her or endure any real or pseudo-crushes, but she reminded him of a brainteaser he wanted to solve.

Waving at a guard, Nicholas ambled the rest of the way to the kitchen, grabbed a couple bottles of water and made the return trip. He paused at the hallway to Tara's room and followed an itchy sensation that led to her doorway. Light shone from underneath the door.

He raised his eyebrows. Why would Miss York be awake at 3:00 a.m.? He leaned closer to the door and heard her voice, then an electronic beep, followed by an oath.

Unable to stifle his curiosity, he tapped on the door. "Miss York," he said.

He heard the patter of her feet on the floor and a thump, followed by another oath.

Ouch. Nicholas winced. Sounded like a stubbed toe.

She cracked the door open and one blue eye peeked out at him. "What do you want?"

"I was up getting some bottled water, saw the light under your door and wondered if you needed some help."

"I'm fine," she said, still keeping the door minutely cracked.

"Is your toe bleeding?" he asked.

She paused, then he saw her hair cover his view of her. "Just a little," she admitted.

"Let me see," he said.

"It's not necessary," she said, a tinge of panic leaking into her voice.

"I'll make that determination. I'm a medical doctor, remember?"

"But—"

Nicholas gently but firmly pushed open the door.

Tara gave a muffled squeak of protest before she jumped out of the way.

Nicholas immediately glanced at her bleeding toe, then bent down and wrapped his hand around her ankle. Tara grabbed the dresser for balance.

"It doesn't look like it will need stitches," he said. "Nasty bruise, though."

Still holding her ankle, he allowed his gaze to travel up her shapely bare legs to the inviting hint of creamy thighs exposed by the high hem of her nightshirt. The nightshirt gave just a few hints of the female form beneath: the curve of her hip and the imprint of her nipples against the pink material.

Farther up, he took in the nervous swallow of her bare throat, then rosebud lips that somehow managed to look like a combination of innocence and sin. Her hair fell over her shoulders like rich cognac.

He looked into her blue eyes, then glanced at the desk where the computer sat with its cursor blinking. No glasses next to the computer. He looked at the bedside table. No glasses.

Suspicion and curiosity vied for supremacy in his mind. Just as he'd thought, Tara York wasn't exactly what she seemed.

Tara bit her lip and pointed at her toe. "See? No big deal. I've got oodles of bandages in my toiletry kit. Are you satisfied?"

Not by a long shot, Nicholas thought. But he would be.

Two

The man was kneeling at her foot and he was half-naked.

"You can let go of my ankle now," Tara said. *So I can think again.* Just the way his fingers looped around her ankle like a bracelet made her edgy. She'd felt his assessing gaze over every inch of her. It reminded her of the one time she'd sunbathed in the nude and gotten a whopper of a burn in tender places. There was no sun in sight at the moment, however, and she was clothed, so Nicholas shouldn't be affecting her tender places one iota.

He squeezed her ankle, then released it. Grabbing the water bottles he'd set on the floor, he stood. "Let's get a bandage on it."

Her heart pounding double time, she went to the

bathroom, foraged in her toiletry bag and grabbed one of her boxes of bandages. She pulled one out and returned to her bedroom.

Before she could apply the bandage, Nicholas snatched it from her fingers and took care of the task himself. "There," he said, rising again and nodding toward her computer. "Problems?"

"I'm having trouble connecting to the Internet," she admitted, relieved to have his attention pulled away from her. She wondered if he had any idea how distracting his bare chest was. "I got the connection number for Marceau before I left home, but it doesn't seem to be working."

"Let me see," he said, striding toward the desk. "I know a few things about computers. Michelina's been calling me His Royal Geekness for years."

That was difficult for Tara to imagine. Nicholas might be intelligent, but he seemed to have all the necessary social skills, and there was certainly nothing nerdlike about his appearance.

"Nice machine," he said, studying the screen. "I see your problem. You don't have the entire prefix. Here," he said, entering two additional numbers. "Try it now."

Tara signed on and was immediately connected. Gratitude rushed through her. "Thank you," she told Nicholas warmly. I've been wrestling with this all night," she said.

He nodded. "No problem. Mind answering a question?"

She did mind, but since he'd solved her computer

dilemma, the least she could do was be polite. "No."

"Why do you wear glasses when you don't need them?"

He'd caught her. Tara felt heat rise to her cheeks. She looked away and took a careful breath. Darn, what could she do now?

"How do you know I don't need them?" she asked, stalling.

"You're not wearing them and they're nowhere in sight. As you say in America, the jig's up."

Tara frowned and looked at him hard. Except for the fact that he was half-nude, he appeared to be a reasonable man. She wondered if she could trust him. "I suppose you'd like the truth," she said reluctantly.

"And nothing but…so help you God as you Americans say." He said it playfully, but she knew he meant the words.

She sighed, irritated that Nicholas was obviously too smart to be taken in by her disguise. "I'm sure you know the purpose of my visit to Marceau is to make a match between you and me. My father wants me to get married. I don't."

"Why don't you?"

"Because I value my independence. I don't want anyone telling me what to do and when to do it," she said bluntly.

He nodded slowly. "Fair enough, but you still haven't told me why you wear glasses when you don't need them."

"I was trying to impress you with my homeliness."

Nicholas blinked, then his lips twitched with humor. "So, what you're telling me is that you deliberately made yourself less attractive so I wouldn't fall under your spell."

"Not exactly," Tara said. "Many men would be able to look past a lack of beauty in exchange for whatever they're hoping to gain from my father. So, I not only need to be unattractive physically, but also socially, I need to—"

"Bore the hell out of me," he finished for her.

"Exactly," she said, surprised that he understood.

He chuckled under his breath and shook his head. "So you really don't want to get married," he said, as much to himself as her.

"Not at all," she admitted.

"And the idea of marrying a prince—who happens to be a doctor—doesn't make the idea more appealing," he clarified.

Tara made a face. "Your royal title probably draws the press like flies at a picnic, and it seems to me that a doctor's wife would spend a lot of time alone."

He chuckled again and rubbed his square chin. "I knew there was something different about you the minute I saw you. My mother has tried to match me up with eleven different women, and I've pulled the same tricks you have. I don't shave and I wear a scruffy beard—and for good measure I discuss microbiology during mealtimes."

Amazement ran through her. "Eleven! Maybe you can give me some pointers. I'm only up to number eight." She took a second look at him, noting his haircut and shaven jaw. "But why did you cut your hair for me?"

"I didn't. I did it for my mother. She's had a tough time lately. A family matter. So I thought I should at least try to be outwardly cooperative."

"Weren't you afraid I might fall for you?"

"I was hoping to reason with you. It was a risk, of course. And if that didn't work, I would have treated you to my microbiology discussion."

"What does Marceau want from my father?"

"Now, that's a mixed bag. Many people in Marceau think it would be great for the economy if your father would build a resort here to attract tourists."

"But you don't agree?"

"I'm not crazy about the idea of a ton of tourists, but it might help the economy. Tourism isn't my area," he said with a shrug. "Medicine is."

Tara crossed her arms over her chest thoughtfully. "I can't claim to have a great deal of influence over my father, but I could certainly mention the possibility when I speak with him," she said and gave in to a little of her own curiosity. "Why don't *you* want to get married?"

"I don't want my attention divided right now. I have some important goals, and I don't want to be distracted by family responsibilities."

His candor lifted a weight from her chest. Tara took a deep breath and looked into Nicholas's honest light blue eyes. She could have sworn she felt a click snap between them. She felt it resonate inside her. "I think we understand each other," she said, unable to remember the last time someone had understood her. "We don't really have to pretend anymore."

"Not to each other," he agreed. "But we've both established that there are other interested parties."

Tara nodded. "My father, your mother. I could cut my visit short."

"And we both would get slammed with questions," he said.

"And I would probably be shipped out to number nine," she said, dreading that prospect.

"Or we could create the necessary illusions while you do your thing and I do mine. As long as we show up together every now and then, the situation could work to our advantage. If we give the impression that our parents have reason to hope they'll be successful in their matchmaking, they'll probably leave us alone."

Tara warmed to the idea, which held out the promise of freedom. "As long as we don't give them too much reason to hope."

"Exactly," Nicholas said. Giving a grin that made her stomach dance, he extended his hand. "Deal?"

She allowed his warm palm to enclose hers. "Deal."

He squeezed her hand, then released it. At the same time, Tara let out her breath. Had she been holding it?

He offered her a bottle of water. "We can drink to it."

She smiled. He was safe, she told herself even though her nerve endings were still jumping. After all, Nicholas Dumont offered a handshake and water, not kisses and champagne. So how could there possibly be any danger?

Three days later, Nicholas knocked on Tara's door again. He'd visited three clinics during the last few days and treated several patients. He had no idea what Tara had been doing except that she'd been taking all her meals in her room, which had drawn the attention of the queen.

Tara opened the door and her eyes lit with surprise. "Hi. What's up?"

"We need to talk," he said, and walked into Tara's room. "My mother has learned that you've been taking all your meals in your room, and she's concerned that you and I aren't spending enough time together."

Tara lifted her hair off the back of her neck and rolled her big blue eyes. Her face free of makeup, she wore a tank top designed to keep her cool and any normal man hot. Her shorts revealed slim shapely legs that brought to mind basic needs he hadn't addressed in ages. In her natural state, Tara York was damn easy on the eyes.

"So what do we need to do?"

"There's a charity ball being held at a hotel downtown. My mother insists we attend."

Tara wrinkled her nose with genuine displeasure. "A ball. When?"

"Tonight. We probably don't have to stay the entire time. A few dances and—"

"Dances! I can't dance. I can barely walk without

running into something. Plus, I need to study for—''
She broke off as if she'd revealed far more than she
intended.

"Study for?" he prompted.

"Nothing that would interest you," she said, and
began to pace. "The timing's terrible. If we absolutely have to go, then I'll go. But I can't dance."

Bemused by the degree of her anxiety, Nicholas
studied her. "It can't be that bad. I'm not big on
dancing, but I can waltz on demand."

She shook her head. "You don't understand. My
father calls it my "little problem." A nice person
would call it a coordination deficit. I call it dangerously clumsy. If you put me on the dance floor with
a lot of innocent people, then you'd better make sure
you're well insured, because somebody's bound to get
hurt, and when they learn who I am, they'll sue." She
met his gaze. "I'm not exaggerating. I don't even
drive a car because of it."

Nonplussed, Nicholas rubbed his jaw. "It's that
bad. Have you been checked by a neurologist?"

She waved her hand in dismissal. "I've been
clumsy since I was a child. No waltzing."

Nicholas searched for a solution that would satisfy
appearances and Tara's aversion to dancing. "You
wouldn't have to waltz. Just a slow dance or two. You
could just lean from side to side and I'll do the rest."

She shot him a doubtful look. "No twirling?"

"No twirling," he assured her. He glanced at the
computer. "What are you studying?"

"Nothing that would interest you," she said in a

cool voice that should have affected him like a door in his face. Instead, he grew more curious.

He walked to her desk and scanned the papers. She snatched them up, but not before he glimpsed the subject. "You're studying psychology. The subject matter looks fairly advanced, not basic stuff."

She cradled the papers to her chest protectively. "It better be advanced. It's my thesis."

Nicholas did a double take. She'd surprised him again. "You're working on your master's degree?"

She gave a small nod.

"What university?"

"I'm getting it on the Internet," she said with great reluctance. "I would appreciate you not telling anyone. My father doesn't know and—"

"Why not?"

She shrugged. "My father is incredibly overprotective. He didn't want me to go to college, and to be perfectly honest, when I first started, I didn't have a lot of confidence. But I've done fine, and I know that if I continue to do well, I'll have more say over what I do with my life."

Nicholas suspected she was playing down her success. "What do you mean by doing fine?"

"I've successfully earned two undergraduate degrees, one in sociology, the other in psychology. I'm two-thirds of the way through my master's degree," she said slowly, as if her disclosure was as painful as pulling teeth.

"Why haven't you told your father?"

"It's not the right time," she said. "Plus I don't

want any criticism or discouragement. I don't want to hear one disparaging word about my field of study, and I know him. He's a businessman, so he would tell me I'm training for a career where all I'll say is 'Do you want fries with that?' There may be some truth to his opinion, but I don't want to hear it right now. I feel better than ever about myself because of this. And I'm not going to let anyone take that away from me.''

The combination of her passion and vulnerability resonated deeply with him. Nicholas had launched an uphill battle to study medicine. Such a thing 'just wasn't done' by members of the royal family, he'd been told over and over again ad nausem. ''Your secret's safe with me. I took a lot of resistance from the royal advisors and the queen as I pursued my own goals. In the end, your father will probably come around. It took my mother a while to get used to the idea of her son becoming a doctor, but now she mentions it every chance she can,'' he added wryly.

Tara smiled. ''My son, the doctor.''

He nodded. ''Yeah.''

He looked into her blue eyes for a long moment and felt a strange sensation in his gut, rather as though he were just remembering he'd skipped a meal and were feeling hungry. He liked her smile, he liked her passion for independence and something about her made him want her to trust him and confide in him. Damned if he knew what it was, he thought ruefully, then returned his attention to the woman in front of him. "Eight o'clock, tonight then. In the foyer. Do you need to shop?"

She gave a mysterious smile and shook her head. "Oh, no, I brought the perfect dress."

At eight-fifteen, Nicholas paced the formal foyer. If Tara weren't in the palace, he'd halfway suspect he was being stood up. Although it was refreshing that he wasn't being chased, he felt a surprising poke at his masculine ego from Tara's complete lack of interest. The completely divergent emotions irritated the hell out of him. Ditching the waiting game, he told the escort and bodyguards to take a break while he checked on Tara.

He knocked on her door several times, but there was no answer. A ripple of concern oozed through him. He wondered if something was wrong. He pushed open the door. "Tara?"

The connecting bathroom door whipped open, and Tara walked out in a rush of steam, wearing only a towel.

Her hair was wet from the shower, and drops of water dotted the swells of her creamy breasts. Nicholas's mouth went dry.

Her eyes widened. "Oh! I'm so sorry. I was studying and I lost track of time. Unforgivably rude, but I hope you'll forgive me," she said, turning to pull a pair of silk bikini panties and a lace bra from her drawer. "I can probably be ready in ten minutes if I rush."

She appeared unaware of the fact that she was com-

pletely naked beneath that towel; Nicholas could
think of nothing else. His body temperature cranked
upward. He wondered if her nipples were pink or
dusky-colored. He wondered how they would feel in
his hands, in his mouth.

Her gaze met his. "Well," she said with a contrite
expression. "Are you angry and offended?"

"No," he said. "Distracted" was a more accurate
description of his mood. "I was just starting to wonder."

She gave a deep sigh of relief, drawing his gaze to
her breasts. Nicholas couldn't help wishing the damn
towel would slip. He transferred his gaze to her legs,
and a steamy visual of settling himself between her
thighs and— He mentally broke off the thought. He
needed a drink. "We'll meet in the foyer in fifteen
minutes. Although I've never met a woman who can
get ready for a ball in that amount of time."

Tara's lips stretched in a smile with an edge of
mischief. "Then I guess it's time you did."

Twelve minutes later, Tara lifted the hem of her
yellow and brown gown as she made her way down
the hall. The dress was both hideous and too big. Her
ensemble felt like a burden tonight. Her glasses
perched on her nose, and she felt a trickle of water
running down her back from her braid. Although she
knew her ruse was no longer necessary for Nicholas,
she suspected it was best to continue her ugly duck-
ling routine in public.

Turning a corner, she met Nicholas's gaze and felt

him dissect her appearance millimeter by millimeter. Her stomach took a crazy dip. If she didn't know better, she'd think he was mentally stripping the yellow and brown gown from her body. But that wasn't possible, she assured herself. Nicholas didn't view her as a sexually attractive woman, just as she didn't view him as a sexually attractive male.

The latter part of her thought process caused a discordant bell to clang inside her head, but she pushed it aside. "Under fifteen minutes," she said. "The only problem is my hair isn't dry, but that's a small price to pay for the extra study time. Are you ready to get this over with?" she asked gamely.

He shook his head. "Your transformation is amazing. Where did you find this…?" He pointed at the dress as if there were no words.

"Easy. I once had my colors done, and I was told which were the best colors for me to wear and which were the worst. This combination of yellow and brown is—"

"The worst," he finished for her.

Tara smiled. "Exactly."

He lifted his gaze from her dress to her eyes and she felt a strange tug in her stomach. Hunger, she told herself.

"Can you take the glasses off when we're alone?"

Her breath stopped in her throat. "Why?"

"Because I ask it."

The hint of regal authority in his voice amused her at the same time that his request unsettled her, but she couldn't really think of a good reason to refuse him. "Okay," she said with a shrug, and slipped her glasses from her face. She wondered how she could feel so naked when her body was covered from neck to toe.

Nicholas extended his arm to her. "The ball awaits."

Three

———

Tara had been dreading this moment the entire evening. Perhaps her entire life. Watching the swirl of evening dresses as tuxedo-dressed men spun their graceful partners around the ballroom, she felt her stomach twist and spin. She could feel a disaster coming. She shouldn't care that she was innately clumsy and that her feet seemed to have a will of their own, with the worst timing imaginable. She shouldn't care that she was probably going to step on Nicholas's well-shined black shoes and fall flat on her face. She shouldn't be embarrassed because she shouldn't care what Nicholas thought of her.

But she did. Just a little bit, Tara insisted to herself, and the reason she cared was because Nicholas wasn't like the others. He wasn't pretending to like her or to be attracted to her.

The music stopped and the orchestra eased into a slow, bluesy tune. Tara felt Nicholas's gaze on her, and her heart tripped.

"Ready?" he asked, sliding his hand down her arm to lace his fingers through hers.

The simple taking of her hand made something inside her jolt. She took a deep breath. "I guess," she said.

Nicholas gently tugged her toward the dance floor. "Smile. You look like you're headed for the guillotine. It's just a dance."

"Easy for you to say," she muttered under her breath, as she moved into dance position. Left hand on his broad shoulder, her right hand captured in his. She felt his other hand at her back, securely drawing her closer.

He began to sway. "Just lean into me. I'll do the work."

Tara lifted her gaze above Nicholas's strong chin, and the light from the chandeliers danced in her peripheral vision, creating an aura behind Nicholas's head. Feeling her equilibrium start to slip, she tightened her fingers on his shoulder and quickly shifted her focus to Nicholas's eyes.

"Problem?" he asked, pulling her closer.

Her chest tightened, making it difficult for her to breathe. "Just a little dizzy," she said, willing the sensation to leave her alone. "You have quite extraordinary eyes. They're so light, they look almost silver.''

"Family characteristic. How long have you had the problem with balance?"

"Since I was about eleven or twelve."

"Do you experience nausea with it?"

"No. When I was younger, I remember often feeling as if someone were moving things like the floor or the steps," she said, smiling wryly.

He chuckled, a low, deep sound that skittered down her nerve endings. "Broken bones?"

"A few. My father couldn't handle me getting hurt. I think he gave the bodyguards instructions to protect me from myself as much as anyone else. If you're trying to find a medical condition in this, you're going to be sorry. It's a very simple diagnosis. Clumsiness. It's inconvenient, but not terminal as long as I'm careful."

Uncomfortable with his undivided attention so focused on her "little problem," Tara looked away from Nicholas's intent gaze. "How much longer do we need to do this?"

"Just until the song ends. Are you afraid I'll let you fall?"

"No," she said in a low voice. Tara knew he wouldn't let her fall, but she couldn't deny her uneasiness about other things, such as the subtle but delicious scent of his aftershave. He was holding her too closely, she thought, but she knew his motivation was protective, not sexual. That didn't change the fact that she was too aware of her breasts pressed against his chest and his hips brushing intimately against her.

The sensation of Nicholas surrounding her with his body and arms kicked up a riot of new and disconcerting feelings inside her. Her breasts felt swollen and her thighs trembled.

Frowning, Tara tried to make sense of it all. She jerked the wrong way and tried to steady herself. Her foot slammed down smartly on his shoe.

Aghast, she looked into his face and caught the slight wince of pain. Misery and embarrassment shot though her. "I'm so sorry, but I did warn you."

He shook his head. "It was nothing."

Tara's stomach knotted. "Yes, it was. Don't lie. The chivalrous routine is totally unnecessary with me."

"I'm not being chivalrous. I'm telling the truth," he insisted, drawing her stiff body against him. "Now, it might have been a different story if you'd been wearing heels. In that case, I might need stitches." His lips twitched. "And perhaps a tetanus shot. If you hit an artery, I might need a blood transfusion. The worst case scenario is if I were to develop a septic infection and need to have the foot amputated or die," he said without a blink. "I think I'll live."

Torn between amusement and her lingering embarrassment, she stared at him for a long moment. "You have an odd sense of humor, Nicholas."

"It distracted you, though, didn't it? You're not holding up your end very well," he told her.

"My end of what? I told you I couldn't dance."

"You're supposed to look like you're enjoying yourself, Tara. Instead, you look as if I'm torturing you."

"Aren't you?" she asked, but couldn't hold back a smile.

His gaze darkened mysteriously, almost sensually, she thought, but told herself the latter was impossible.

"There's a thin line between pleasure and pain. If I were going to torture you, I'd choose a more private setting. Relax," he coaxed. "You're as stiff as a board."

She groaned and deliberately tried to soften her stance. "It's tough to relax when you're talking about pleasure and pain while a hundred people are waiting to watch me fall on my face."

"You're majoring in psychology. Use a mind trick. Pretend I'm your dream man."

Tara's mind went completely blank. "I don't think I have a dream man."

Nicholas made a tsking sound. "Sounds like a bad case of denial."

"Okay, then who is your dream woman?"

"My dream woman is one who doesn't want to marry me and who won't prevent me from pursuing my interests."

"That could be your sister," Tara said.

It was Nicholas's turn to groan. "Add passion, intelligence and great legs."

"You want a great lover," Tara clarified, feeling a mixture of relief and the faintest pinch of inadequacy. She was completely sexually inexperienced, so that put her out of the running for Nicholas's dream woman. That was good, she told herself, and thanked the heavens when the music finally stopped. She immediately pulled away, wanting to rub away his disturbing effect on her. "Duty accomplished," she said, fighting breathlessness. "We can leave now."

Two hours later, Tara was safely situated in her room with her textbook on advanced bio-psychology preparing for an all-nighter of study. Nicholas would prefer a different kind of all-nighter with his so-called dream woman, she thought. An image of heat, nakedness and need slithered through her mind, and she shook her head.

Tara forced her mind to focus on the subject at hand. Before she knew it, another two hours passed, and then there was a knock at her door. Her heart hammered in surprise. She padded toward the door and wrapped her hand around the knob. "Who is it?"

"Nicholas. With sustenance," he added. "I couldn't sleep, and I saw the light under your door when I went to the kitchen."

She opened the door, prepared to send him on his way. The tray of sandwiches, cookies and coffee he carried, however, reminded her that she'd never eaten dinner. She told herself she would eat and send him away, and she absolutely would not look at his bare chest or legs. Geez, didn't the man own a robe or something?

"Thank you," she said. "I forgot I was hungry until now."

"No problem," he said, setting the tray down on a table by the bed. "I was awake."

"Do you suffer from insomnia frequently?" she asked.

"Just when I have unsolved mysteries on my mind," he said, grabbing half a sandwich and taking a bite as he sank onto her bed.

Tara took a half sandwich for herself. "What sort of unsolved mysteries?"

He swallowed and shrugged. "How to fund the free clinics I want to start for some of the more remote areas of Marceau. I think I can recruit volunteer physicians to donate time on a monthly or bimonthly basis, but supplies and treatment will require funding. Since I'm royalty, it wouldn't look right if I got the money from the government. Plus there would be too many strings attached."

"You probably need to set up some sort of charitable foundation or find a sponsor," Tara suggested.

He nodded. "And that's not my area. Medicine is."

She took a bite and returned to her spot on the bed. "You said *mysteries*. Is there more than one?"

He nodded again, his face turning serious. "Can you keep a secret?"

"Yes. Why?"

"We don't want to get the press involved yet."

"I avoid the press."

He took another bite and swallowed it. "This is about my brother."

"Which one?"

He gave a faint smile. "Good question. My youngest brother died in a boating accident when he was three years old.''

Tara felt an instant surge of sympathy. ''That's terrible. I didn't know.''

''It's not something my family has spent a lot of time discussing. Freud would have a field day with it,'' he said wryly. ''But that's for another day. We have reason to believe that he didn't actually die in the boating accident.''

Tara did a double take. ''Why?''

''We received a letter with a lock of his hair and a button from the jacket he was wearing at the time he fell overboard. We were taking a family vacation in Bermuda. My uncle took a few of us out one afternoon on his sailboat, and a terrible storm came up out of nowhere. We couldn't get back in time and were stuck out there half the night. The boat nearly tipped over. My brother fell overboard. There were massive searches, but he was never found. It nearly destroyed my parents.''

Tara shook her head. ''What an amazing story. Do you have any idea what could have happened to him?''

''Some ideas, but nothing solid. We've got detectives on it. The DNA from the hair matches the Dumonts'.''

Tara tried to imagine losing a child, then being teased with the prospect of regaining him. ''Your mother must be…''

Nicholas nodded. ''She's putting up a good front, but she's fragile. Even when my father died, she remained strong in front of us. I saw her hands tremble once on the day we buried him. And now, there's a little desperation I see in her eyes every now and then."

"That's why you shaved," she said, liking Nicholas more than ever. "And why you're willing to play along with the idea of entertaining me as a marital prospect."

"For the time being," he said, narrowing his eyes. "It helps that you're as uninterested in getting married as I am. You sure as hell aren't high maintenance. I have to practically drag you out of your room to *entertain* you. What are you studying?" he asked, reaching for her textbook. "Bio-psychology. My area. I can help you study."

"Thanks, but no thanks," Tara said, reaching for the book. She suspected her concentration would go straight down the toilet if he helped her.

He snatched the book to his chest and wagged his finger at her. "One moment, *chérie*. I'm going to check your knowledge."

Tara sighed. "That's what the test is designed to do."

He cracked open the book. "What is dopamine?"

"A substance that transmits messages between nerve cells in the brain. The absence of dopamine has been associated with lack of attention issues and impulsivity."

"Very good," he said. "Dopamine also controls the secretion of growth hormone."

"Show-off," she muttered.

He glanced up at her for a long moment and smiled. "No one has ever called me a show-off before this."

"They were probably afraid they would get their heads chopped off."

"And you're not?" he asked with a hint of sexual challenge in his eyes.

"No, but if it will make you feel better," she said with a mock respectful dip of her head, "show-off, Your Highness."

He chuckled, then glanced back at the book. "Hyperthyroidism," he said.

She couldn't dodge the commanding note in his voice. It was so natural, she wondered if he was aware of it. "Excessive secretion of the thyroid gland that produces accelerated metabolic rate, extreme apprehension and excitability."

"Another thyroid disorder created by underactivity of the thyroid gland is—"

"My—" Tara closed her eyes. The word was on the tip of her tongue. "Myx—"

"Close enough. Myxoedema. Patients are frequently slow and tired—"

"—and overly sensitive to cold. They exhibit a slow pulse and reflexes."

He met her gaze with a glint of respect. She felt a heady rush at his expression. For her, respect had come in small, stingy doses, and she craved more. "Next," she said, lifting her chin in challenge, sensing that generating the glint of respect in Nicholas's striking eyes could become addicting.

Nicholas continued to quiz her for the next hour and a half, and her ability to answer his onslaught built up her confidence.

"Androgens," he said with a sly sideways glance.

She rolled her eyes at his choice. "Sex hormones."

"Testosterone," he prompted.

"The chemical that causes grown men to fight like little boys," she joked, punchy from the late hour and Nicholas's relentless quizzing. "You ought to know."

He set the book down. "How do you know I got into fights?"

"With all those brothers, the testosterone must've run rampant. It's a wonder you didn't kill each other. Besides, your affinity for fencing gives you away.

"Testosterone is the most potent of the naturally occurring androgens. It plays a significant role in dominance and aggression. I appreciate your tutoring," she said. "But you have been dominating my bed for the last couple of hours, and since it's after three in the morning, it's my turn to dominate my own bed."

His gaze fell over her in a wholly masculine way, and Tara had the odd sensation of how Nicholas might look at her if she were a fencing partner. Or bed partner. The notion shimmied down her nerve endings like an electrical current.

He dropped the book beside him and leaned forward. "I think it would be fascinating to watch you dominate in bed."

Alarm and forbidden excitement raced through her.

She cleared her throat and tried to clear her mind.
"Not fascinating at all," she said, lifting her hand as
if she were on the witness stand. "I promise it would
be boring. Just me in my nightshirt under the covers,
breathing evenly, getting my REM sleep, with my
eyes closed. See?" she said, growing increasingly
nervous with each movement as he drew closer to her.
"Boring. Very boring," she said, wishing she didn't
sound so breathless.

He lifted his hand to her chin and rubbed his thumb
over her throat.

She swallowed at the seductive gesture. "What are
you doing?" she whispered.

"Just looking," he said, his eyes a kaleidoscope of
predatory sensuality.

"You're not just looking," she told him in a voice
that could have used a lot more conviction. "You're
touching."

"So I am," he said, sliding his thumb over her
chin, then slowly across her lips. "You're not at all
what I expected."

She wasn't sure if that was good or bad. She only
knew her brain felt as if it were turning to sludge
while he stroked her lips with his thumb. His gaze
slid over her lips like a hot French kiss, then he
looked into her eyes. "I think we should get engaged," he said.

Four

Tara's heart and brain felt as if they had just slammed into a brick wall. She gaped at him, searching for her breath and *his* sanity. She pulled back from his hand and glanced at him suspiciously. "Exactly how long have you been taking mind-altering medication, Your Highness?"

His lips tilted in a crooked grin and he rose from the bed. "My brain is as clear as a bell. This idea is a stroke of genius."

"Which lies very close to madness," she muttered.

"No, it's *genius,*" he insisted. "If you and I become engaged, my mother will get off my back, and I can do what I want to do. Your father will stop husband-shopping for you, and you can do what *you* want to do."

Tara frowned. "Yes, but I think you're forgetting that an engagement normally precedes a wedding, and neither you nor I want to be married."

"Which is solved by an extended engagement," Nicholas said.

"An extended engagement is still followed by a wedding and a marriage," she said, rising from the bed to face him.

"Not necessarily," he said. "Engagements can be broken."

Tara blinked. "Broken," she echoed.

"Of course. After a few years, you can dump my royal ass," he said, warming to the idea as he explained it. "This would be perfect. It would take me off the marriageable bachelor market, which would get the press out of my hair. I would be able to focus on getting my clinics running without distractions."

She shook her head. "I don't think you've thought this all the way through. The engagement itself will cause a media feeding frenzy, and we would be pestered for a wedding date. We would also be forced to make public appearances. It's terrible timing for me."

Nicholas looked down into the alarmed blue-eyed gaze of the woman whom he was certain possessed the intelligence and independence to carry off the charade. "What's your alternative?"

She stared at him for a long moment and sighed. "Prospect number nine," she grumbled. "I could probably delay it with a bad cold or pneumonia. Or I could break another toe. That would be really inconvenient, though."

"An engagement *is* the answer," Nicholas assured her. "We tell my family to keep it secret for a while. Then, when it leaks to the press, we announce a wedding date two years away. When the families start to pressure, we postpone the ceremony for some to-be-determined reason. We might be able to get four or five years of freedom out of this."

"I don't know," she said, looking at him suspiciously. "What about when you meet someone you want to—" Her cheeks colored, and she broke off as if she were searching for the right words. "When you decide you need to—" She broke off again and cleared her throat.

He shook his head. "When I need to what?"

Tara exhaled in frustration, sending a strand of her bangs flying. "When your testosterone kicks in," she said, lifting her chin defiantly.

It occurred to him that in another time he could have demanded her submission in every possible way. The Dumonts weren't known for abusing their royal power, but Nicholas had an inkling that Tara York's independence could drive a man to take extraordinary measures to make her his. Not that he was driven in such a way, he told himself.

"My testosterone," he said. "You mean when I feel the need to fence or start a war for the purpose of world domination?"

She glowered at him. "You know what I mean. When you find someone you want to take as a lover."

His mind wandered, not for the first time, to the

tantalizing image of Tara in bed. Naked, passionate, giving and wanting. "What's the problem?"

"Well, if the press should learn you've taken a lover other than your fiancée, they'll be all over it."

"I can be discreet," he said. "What about you?"

Her eyes widened in surprise, as if the notion hadn't occurred to her. "Um, I—" She shook her head and ran a hand through her hair. "Taking a lover isn't really my top priority. There are other things that are much more important to me right now."

"But everyone has needs, Tara," he said.

She bit her lip and looked as if she'd rarely considered her sexual needs. Then her eyes darkened, as if with sensual secrets, arousing his curiosity. "I'll be discreet."

"Then it's settled," he said. "We're engaged."

Alarm crossed her face. "No, we're *not*. Nothing is settled. I'm not making this kind of decision in the middle of the night."

"It's a no-brainer, *chérie,*" he said, feeling oddly impatient with her reticence.

"Maybe for you," she said. "I need to sleep on this. I need to think about it."

"Why do you find me objectionable as a pretend fiancé?"

She crossed her arms over her chest. "I—I didn't say I found you objectionable. Not you personally, anyway. But I do find the idea of engagement and marriage horrifying."

"But *I* don't offend you with the way I look or act?" he probed.

"For the most part, no," she said slowly, with a great deal of wariness. "I'm sure you know you're good-looking, intelligent and charming when you want to be, Nicholas."

"Then why delay?"

"Because I want to," she said, lifting her chin again.

"That's not rational," he said.

"It's after three o'clock. A half-naked prince has just suggested I become engaged to him. I don't have to be rational."

"Would it help if I were dressed differently?"

"I don't know," she said, rubbing her forehead. "It would help if you left."

Nicholas touched the soft underside of her chin and tilted her head upward. She looked so distressed and lost that an odd tenderness immediately slid through him. He wanted to soothe away the confusion and discomfort he read on her face. He wanted her to trust him. It was a strange, overwhelming need that ate at him. In another century, he could have demanded her compliance. The notion came out of left field. He sure as hell had never considered demanding someone trust him.

"This is going to work out very well," he assured her, rubbing his thumb over her silky bottom lip. He felt a lick of arousal curl in his stomach. "In fact, it could be perfect."

"Nothing's perfect," she whispered, her eyes dark with a combination of wariness and a woman's need denied.

Her expression presented a challenge he couldn't ignore. Nicholas lowered his head. "Have some faith, Tara. You could be surprised."

He took her mouth with his and was surprised at the level of electricity that raced through him. Her lips were soft, warm and inviting. He rubbed his mouth against hers, absorbing every sensation...her delicious, shocked intake of breath, the hint of her sweet taste and the velvet softness of her sensitive inner lips. He couldn't resist sliding his tongue just inside her mouth and swallowing her sigh.

She instinctively curled her lips around his tongue, and he felt himself grow hard with mind-spinning speed. He pulled back and stared at her. "This doesn't have to be all bad."

She licked her lips, and it was all he could do not to groan. He watched her take a deep breath, as if to clear her head. She shook her head. "This is crazy...and *you* are the devil."

The following morning Tara couldn't bear the confinement of her lovely suite. She could hardly bear the confinement of her skin, so she took a walk around the palace grounds. She wondered if she'd dreamed Nicholas's crazy proposition. She prayed she'd dreamed his kiss, but she knew she hadn't.

She'd tossed and turned alternately dreaming of his sensual kiss and of an appalling royal wedding with her as the bride. Tara shuddered at the thought. Every time she imagined herself married, she felt trapped and suffocated. As appealing as Nicholas was, marriage to him would entail even more restrictions than marriage to the average man.

In the bright light of day, his pretend-engagement idea was insane, yet she could see a few benefits. If they could keep the engagement roller coaster from riding out of control into a full-blown marriage, it was possible that she and Nicholas might actually gain some relief from their family pressures. The idea of dealing with the press, however, turned Tara's stomach.

Voices calling in the distance interrupted her thoughts.

"Elvis! Elvis!"

Tara stared in the direction of the voices and saw Prince Michel's wife, Maggie, and son, Max, yelling. "Elvis!"

Elvis? Tara wondered if the entire family was demented. Perhaps there was something in the water?

Maggie waved toward Tara. "We're looking for Elvis," she said, rushing toward her. Max's face was full of distress.

"Elvis," Tara echoed, confused. "Elvis Presley. Isn't he…?"

"No!" Maggie said, her eyes wide with alarm. "Elvis is Max's beagle. Have you seen him?"

Tara shook her head. "No, but I've only been out here a few minutes. Can I help you look for him?"

"Please do. We'll try the pond," Maggie said. "If we don't find him soon, we'll have to enlist the help of the guards. That will get back to the queen."

"And she'll say 'I told you so,'" Max finished. "The queen doesn't like Elvis."

"I don't think she dislikes Elvis. I think his barking makes her nervous," Maggie said.

"And when he pees on the palace floor."

Maggie winced. "Yes, and when he chewed the leg of that sixteenth-century chair." She shrugged. "But puppies do these things."

Tara couldn't help smiling at the odd combination of normalcy and breech of royal protocol. "If I may ask, how did you manage to get the queen to agree to the puppy in the first place?"

"Maggie snookered him in after I memorized my speech for Citizenship Day," Max said proudly.

"Sneaked," Maggie corrected with a smile as she ruffled his cowlick. "Michel was the one who went to bat for us and stuck to his guns," she said, love for her husband glowing from her eyes. "Otherwise, we wouldn't be looking for Elvis right now. He would have been shipped back to the States."

"Elvis!" Max yelled.

Maggie winced. "The guards will be here any minute, but we can't *not* yell."

Wanting to help, Tara lifted her fingers to her lips and let out a loud whistle.

Max did a double take. "Wow."

A dog's bark sounded in the distance, and seconds later a beagle bounded out from the thickly wooded area in the distance.

"Elvis!" Max cried.

Maggie glanced at Tara and smiled. "You've saved

the day. How can we repay you? How about Nicholas on a silver platter with an apple in his mouth?'' she suggested with wicked humor in her eyes.

Tara felt a surge of heat at the mere mention of his name, and immediately shook her head. ''Oh, no. I don't—''

Maggie patted her shoulder. ''It's okay. It's common knowledge that Nicholas can be the most charming man on earth when it suits him. He can also be a major pain if he thinks that mode's in his best interest. Such as when Queen Anna gets matchmaking on the brain.''

Tara couldn't muster one appropriate word, so she moved her head in a noncommittal circle.

''Let's take Elvis back inside,'' Maggie called to Max as the little boy snapped a leash to the beagle's collar. She turned back to Tara as the three walked back toward the palace. ''I hope Nicholas hasn't been too difficult.''

''Not at all,'' Tara said, thinking ''difficult'' was far too mild a term to describe Nicholas. ''He's been a perfect host.''

Maggie looked skeptical.

Tara focused on keeping her balance on the uneven ground to keep from stumbling.

''Go ahead and take Elvis into the basement,'' Maggie told Max, slowing as they neared the palace door.

Max frowned. ''But I wanted to play with him.''

''You can in the basement,'' she said. ''I think we can all use a break from the hot sun.''

Tara glanced over at Maggie, surprised to see that the redhead's complexion had turned white as paper. Alarmed, she moved closer. "Do you need to sit down?"

Maggie gave a little shake of her head and lifted her finger to her lips in a quick secret gesture. "Make sure you give Elvis some water, Max. He's probably thirsty after his adventure. I'll join you in a few minutes, sweetie."

Max sped through the palace door, and Maggie sank to a stone bench just a few steps away. She lowered her head to her hands.

"Should I get Nicholas?" Tara asked, feeling helpless.

"Oh, no," Maggie said, shaking her head.

"Can I get you something to drink?"

Maggie shook her head again. "I just need to take a few deep breaths and cool down."

"Then we should go inside," Tara insisted, worried about the warm, sunny woman she'd so recently met.

"There will be questions and a fuss. I'm not ready for that, yet."

Tara stared down at Maggie in confusion. "Not if you come to my room."

Still pale, Maggie glanced up at her. "Good idea," she said and slowly stood. "Let's go."

It took only a couple of minutes to walk the short distance to Tara's room, but Tara broke into a cold sweat as Maggie leaned on her. She prayed she wouldn't lose her balance. When they arrived, Maggie immediately reclined on Tara's bed and closed her eyes.

"Are you sure I shouldn't get Nicholas?" Tara asked, wishing the color would return to Maggie's face.

"Very sure," she said, then sighed. "Can you keep a secret?"

Tara nodded. After all, her life was full of secrets. What was one more? "Yes," she said.

Maggie opened her eyes and smiled. "I'm pregnant," she whispered.

Even from three feet away, Tara could feel Maggie's warm joy. "How exciting. I'm sure Prince Michel is thrilled."

Maggie's smile dipped. "Well, he doesn't exactly know yet."

Tara blinked in disbelief. "He doesn't?"

Maggie's eyes darkened with a trace of guilt. "I'll tell him soon. As soon as I tell him, though, he'll monitor every move I make, every bite I eat. He's incredibly fussy about my health and safety. He gets upset when I get a splinter."

Tara felt a surprising twinge of longing to be loved so passionately, then wondered where the odd feeling had come from. "He obviously loves you very much."

"Yes, he does," Maggie said, her voice softening. "When we met, I wasn't in the market for a husband, let alone a husband who was going to be king, but he changed my mind." She glanced up at Tara. "The

Dumonts have a habit of changing other people's minds.''

Tara thought of Nicholas's ridiculous proposal and felt her stomach clench. *Not mine,* she told herself. ''Since Elvis is living at the palace, it sounds as if you've influenced things around here too.''

''A little,'' Maggie conceded. She glanced around the room, and her gaze landed on the desk. ''I see you brought your laptop. Do you work for your father?''

Tara couldn't suppress a laugh. ''Not likely. My father is very controlling, and he still views me as a ten-year-old.''

Maggie nodded understandingly and slowly sat up. ''He wants you to get married so you'll be safe and protected.''

Tara felt a knot of self-consciousness well up in her throat. ''He might as well take out a classified ad. I think everyone in the world knows that my father wants me to get married.''

Maggie's lips tilted in a wry smile. ''If it helps, you're not alone. Queen Anna wants all of her children married and producing heirs. Right now, Nicholas is numero uno on her hit list.''

A knock sounded on the bedroom door, and Tara opened it to Nicholas. Her heart jumped at the determination in his gaze. He took her hand and lifted it to his lips. ''So, *ma chérie,* have you decided to accept my proposal?''

Five

"**M**y, oh, my. Nicholas works a lot faster than I would have imagined."

Tara heard Maggie's teasing voice over the roaring in her ears and cringed. She glared at Nicholas. "No," she said, pulling their joined hands away from his lips. "Nicholas isn't talking about that kind of proposal," she said, her eye twitching at the untruth. "He's talking about taking me on an outing. He wants to impress me with the island, so I'll encourage my father to build a resort here," she said, uncomfortably aware of the fact that she was fabricating and not doing it well. She squeezed his hand. "Right?"

He lifted an eyebrow and glanced at Maggie, then back to Tara. "Right. We're going to the Westwood Beach."

Tara tugged her hand away from his and rubbed it against her side as she turned to face Maggie. "That's right. Westwood Beach. We just need to arrange the time, and I need to make sure I have my sunscreen."

Maggie slid a skeptical glance over Nicholas. "Make sure you take plenty of sunscreen. Westwood is a topless beach."

Tara restrained herself from stepping on his foot. Instead, she worked at producing a smile. "I only brought a one-piece swimsuit with me."

"The palace has a selection of swimsuits—"

Tara tossed Nicholas a drop-dead look for his helpfulness.

He shrugged. "But you should wear whatever makes you most comfortable." He turned to Maggie. "I haven't seen you around much. You look a little pale. Everything okay?"

Annoyingly observant, Tara added to Nicholas's character description.

"I'm fine. I've just been busy with your brother and nephew," Maggie said, standing, and gazing back and forth at Nicholas and Tara. "Tara and I were just discussing what the two of you have in common."

"Oh, really. What's that?" he asked.

"Her father wants her to get married. Your mother wants you to get married."

"You left out the most important common denominator," Tara quickly added. "Neither Nicholas nor I want to get married."

Maggie nodded skeptically and walked toward the door. "Uh-huh. Well, I should get back to Max. I've enjoyed chatting with you, Tara. Don't be a stranger. It's nice having another American in the palace.''

As soon as Maggie closed the door behind her, Tara rounded on Nicholas. "*Why* did you do that? Now, she's going to think something is going on between you and me, and nothing is.''

"That could change." Nicholas's lips twitched. "Especially if we go to Westwood Beach.''

Tara rolled her eyes. "We're not going to a nude beach," she told him.

"Westwood's only topless. If you prefer a nude beach, it's a little more of a drive, but—''

Tara wanted to scream. "I don't want to go to a nude beach! I don't want to go to any beach with you.''

"Well, you have to now," Nicholas said.

"Why?''

"Because you told her we were going to the beach. We'll sit down to dinner, and Maggie will ask you how the beach was, and it will get deathly quiet while everyone waits for you to respond. If you say we didn't go, everyone will wonder why not." He inclined his head toward her. "It would have been a lot easier if you'd just told her we were getting engaged.''

"Easier for whom?" Tara asked in disbelief.

"For both of us. See, if you said we're engaged, then everyone will be excited. They might ask you questions, but I could tell them you're overwhelmed with joy and they shouldn't badger you.''

"How long have you been delusional?" Tara asked dryly.

"I'm not delusional. I'm right. This is perfect."

"But I don't want to marry you, and you don't want to marry me."

He pointed his index finger at her. "And that's why it's perfect. I won't get in your way. You won't get in mine."

He made it all sound so practical, so logical, yet Tara knew the situation was fraught with complications. Plus, Nicholas made her nervous. She feared he had the ability to kiss the stuffing out of her with no emotional consequences to himself. She bit her lip. "I just don't know you well enough to pretend to be engaged to you."

He gave a long-suffering sigh and rubbed his hand through his hair. "Okay. How about if I take you on a secret outing tomorrow? It will reveal more about me."

"I'm not going to a nude beach with you."

He chuckled. "This isn't a nude beach. You have to wear clothes, and you have to pretend I'm not a Dumont."

She felt intrigued, despite her reservations. "Where would we go?"

"It's a surprise," he said firmly.

"I want to know," she returned just as firmly.

"And you will. Tomorrow."

Tara tamped down her frustration. "But how should I dress?"

"Casual," he said. "How'd you do on your test?"

Tara blinked at the change in subject. "I haven't taken it yet."

"Why not?"

Tara resisted the urge to squirm beneath his intense gaze. *Because you rattled my brain so that I can't think straight.* "I just haven't."

"You know the material," he said, and his easy yet complete confidence in her knowledge took her breath away. No one had ever expressed such belief in her.

She couldn't speak for an entire moment. "Thank you," she finally managed.

He wrinkled his brow in confusion. "For what?"

She shrugged, not wanting to explain. "Just thank you. What time tomorrow?"

He shook his head as if he still didn't get it. "I'll never understand the way women think," he muttered. "Nine o'clock in the morning. It's a day trip. I'll ask the kitchen staff to pack a lunch for us."

Dismay shot through her. "A whole day?"

He chuckled at her lack of enthusiasm. "Be careful. Your excitement will make me think you're crazy about me."

"But the whole day," she repeated.

"Take your exam and get it out of the way," he advised her, then snagged her hand and lifted it to his lips.

Unnerved, she batted his hand aside. "You need to stop doing that."

"You need to get used to it, *ma chérie. A bientôt,*" he said.

"A bientôt," she echoed, making a face at the door. Under her breath, she muttered, *"Ma chérie,* my fanny. I am nobody's *chérie,* and least of all His Royal Sneakiness's *chérie."*

That evening at a formal family dinner, Tara endured another battery of questions from the queen. Maggie chimed in with the news that Nicholas was taking Tara to the beach. Michelina offered to take Tara swimsuit shopping.

Nicholas covered his chuckle with a cough. "Where were you thinking of taking Tara shopping?" he asked Michelina.

"I'm sure Tara would enjoy a quick trip to Paris," she said in wide-eyed innocence. "Or Beverly Hills."

Queen Anna shook her head in disapproval. "Absolutely not. We have several fine boutiques in Marceau. There's no reason to drag Miss York off the island for such a frivolous reason."

"Perhaps she would enjoy a little getaway," Michelina said, squaring off against her mother.

"Michelina, not everyone feels the necessity to escape Marceau. In fact, many people treasure the opportunity to visit our island."

Michelina lifted her chin. Nicholas could see trouble brewing with his sister. It wouldn't be long before some sort of explosion occurred between her and his mother.

"I think we should ask Tara what she thinks. After all, she is our guest," Michelina said. "Would you like a little getaway, Tara?"

Nicholas watched Tara's eyes round with dismay. It was clear that she was being placed square in the middle of a power play between the queen and Michelina. The room grew hushed with expectation. She looked from his mother to his sister and cleared her throat. "Marceau is a beautiful place, and it has so much to offer. I can see why someone would visit and never want to leave."

Her comments drew a smile of approval from the queen.

"On the other hand, it's quite natural for people who have spent their lives in one place to want to explore other places."

The queen's smile faded.

"I actually think it's a sign of good upbringing. It takes confidence to be willing to venture away from home."

Silence followed. Détente between his mother and Michelina. "Very well done," Nicholas murmured for her ears only. "Are you sure you don't have political aspirations?"

Tara gave him a sideways glance. She opened her mouth to speak, but a palace aide strode to her side. "Please forgive the interruption, Miss York, but you have a visitor in the west parlor."

Tara looked at the aide in surprise. "A visitor?"

"Yes. Mr. Richard Worthington III."

Chagrin and dismay covered her face. "Dickie?" she echoed weakly.

"Who is Dickie?" Nicholas couldn't help asking.

She met his gaze and gave a deep sigh. "Number seven," she whispered.

"I thought you were done with number seven."

"I thought I was too. He was especially persistent."

"What shall I tell Mr. Worthington?" the aide asked.

"Tell him to take a slow boat to Alaska," Nicholas suggested.

"No," she said, biting her lip. "He's traveled very far. The least I can do is see him. Tell him I'll be out in a few minutes." She turned to the rest of the dinner party. "Thank you for the lovely meal and company. Please excuse me. I need to leave."

No excuses. Just *I need to leave.* Nicholas admired her style. He watched her rise from her chair and immediately decided to join her. "Same with me," he said. "Thanks, I need to go."

Queen Anna arched an eyebrow. "Why?"

"Because my guest is leaving," he said. "Good night."

As soon as the two of them left the formal dining room, Tara turned to him. "You didn't need to come."

"I want to size up my competition," he said, tongue-in-cheek.

Tara rolled her eyes and groaned. "If my father were broke, this wouldn't be happening."

"But he's not, and it is," Nicholas reminded her cheerfully. "I've been dealing with the same kind of thing my entire life. No use whining."

"I wasn't whining," she said.

"No?"

"I was complaining."

His lips twitched. "Thanks for making that distinction."

She nodded and adjusted her thick glasses. "Do I look homely enough to discourage Dickie?"

Although her glasses annoyed the hell out of him, her hair was twisted in some kind of unattractive bun and her shapeless brown dress hid her curves, Nicholas couldn't forget what was behind her disguise. The eyes behind those glasses glinted with humor, intelligence and feminine secrets. When she wore her hair down, it begged for a man's touch. And her body could drive a man to distraction.

"Depends how astute he is," he finally said.

"What do you mean?"

"I mean you can put Godiva chocolates in a plain box, but when you take a bite, there's no hiding the fact that the chocolate's Godiva."

Tara frowned. "He's not getting close enough to take a bite out of me. Let's go and get this over with," she said, and they walked the short distance to the west parlor.

As soon as Tara entered the room, Dickie sprang from his seat on the couch and rushed toward her. Tara drew back, but Dickie didn't seem to notice as he enveloped her in an embrace. Nicholas didn't have experience assessing other men's appeal, but he suspected his sister might describe Dickie as a hunk.

Number seven was tall and muscular, with a handsome, if desperate, face.

"Oh, Tara, I've missed you terribly. I can't believe I let you get away."

"Your company's merger with one of my father's companies fell through."

Dickie's face fell and he drew back slightly. "Yes, but—"

Tara took advantage of the moment and took a giant step away from him. "I'm sorry. I did mention it to my father, but I've never had a great deal of influence with him when it comes to business," Tara said. "Please allow me to introduce His Highness, Nicholas Dumont."

Dickie reluctantly transferred his attention to Nicholas. He nodded. "Your Highness. Your country is lovely."

"Yes, it is. As is Tara," he said, sliding his arm around Tara's waist, ignoring her start of surprise. "She and I have become very close during her visit here."

Dickie narrowed his eyes. "I can understand that, she's easy to fall for. But Tara and I share a special history," he said with forced affection.

"Really?"

"We attended kindergarten together," Tara said, subtly trying to wiggle out of Nicholas's arm.

"How sweet," Nicholas said. "But as you can see, she's all grown-up now."

Dickie frowned. "Yes, and Tara and I have an understanding between ourselves."

"Really?" Nicholas repeated, his voice full of deliberate skepticism.

"Yes," Dickie said with challenge in his eyes. He nodded toward Tara. "Tell him about us, Tara."

"Tell him what?" she asked.

Dickie looked at her in surprise. "I know you haven't forgotten that I told you of my intention to marry you."

Nicholas heard the sound of footsteps entering the parlor.

"Hello," Maggie called. "I understand we have another Yank in the palace. Michel and I thought we'd pop in."

Nicholas glanced over his shoulder and saw curiosity on Maggie's face. His brother Michel looked as if he'd been dragged along. "Your Highness," he said to Michel.

Michel lifted a brow at Nicholas's formality.

"This is my brother, His Highness, Michel Dumont, heir to the throne, and his wife, Princess Maggie," Nicholas announced, and mentally added trumpets in the background. "Your Highness, this is one of Tara's friends from America, Dickie."

Dickie stretched his neck against his collar in discomfort, then gave a nod of respect. "Your Highnesses," he mumbled.

"It's a pleasure to meet one of Tara's friends," Maggie said.

Dickie nodded again. "Thank you," he said, then turned back to Nicholas and Tara. "As I was saying, Tara and I have an understanding."

"Strange," Nicholas said, tightening his arm slightly as he heard more footsteps enter the room. "Tara and I have more than an understanding."

She shot him a look of wary dismay.

"We're engaged to be married," Nicholas said.

Tara's gasp was overshadowed by the collective gasps of the other occupants of the room.

"That's incredible," he heard his sister, Michelina, say from behind him.

"God has answered my prayers," Queen Anna crowed.

Tara stared at Nicholas with a mixture of horror and anger.

Red with indignation, Dickie stretched his neck against his collar again. "Well, Tara, is this true?" he demanded in an injured voice that Nicholas hoped Tara wouldn't fall for. "I thought you and I had shared something special. Do you want this prince you've just met, or do you want me, a man you knew even when you were a child?"

Tara bit her lip, her gaze moving between Dickie and Nicholas as if she were trying to choose between two forms of torture. She looked as if she wanted to punch Nicholas.

Her moment of indecision stretched, and Nicholas began to sweat. That was strange, he thought. He and Tara would have a mutually beneficial arrangement, and he would love to take her to bed, but he wasn't capable of anything involving his emotions at the moment.

She gave a heavy sigh, still looking as if she were

choosing between two devils. "Nicholas was correct. He and I are engaged."

Nicholas felt a rush of victory with a tinge of primitive possessiveness he would examine later. Following instinct, he pulled her into his arms and took her mouth with his. He swallowed her gasp of surprise and lingered over her soft lips. He felt her clutch his arms as if she weren't sure whether to push him away or hang on for dear life.

"You've made me a happy man," he said, and saw the dual meaning registered in her eyes. He could tell she knew he was saying the words for the benefit of their audience. At the same time, he was delighted to get his mother off his back, even if only temporarily. He and Tara shared a secret, and it wrapped around them like a silken rope, binding them together.

She leaned closer as if to tuck her head into his shoulder for protection. "If this turns out badly," she said in a sexy, intimate whisper, "I will make your life a living hell."

Six

"Another wedding," Michelina said, sliding her hands together in delight.

Tara stiffened and looked at Nicholas's beautiful sister. She could see endless shopping and whirlwind makeover written all over Michelina's face.

"I'm so pleased, Nicholas," Queen Anna said, moving toward Nicholas and embracing him.

Tara blinked. It was the first time she'd seen Queen Anna give anyone a hug. Her uneasiness escalated to pure panic. Queen Anna must really want her son married off.

Tara cleared her throat and caught Nicholas's gaze with a sharp glare. She noticed that Dickie must have slid out of the room during Nicholas's mind-robbing kiss.

"We don't want to move too fast," he said, giving his mother a quick hug. "Tara is overwhelmed, and I promised her I would give her time to adjust to Marceau and my life before rushing into a wedding."

Michelina's face fell. The queen's followed. "How much adjustment time before you plan to set a date?" Queen Anna Catherine demanded.

"At least six months," he said, holding up his hand before she could protest. "And we plan to hold off telling the press."

"But why on earth would you wait that long before you set a date?" the queen asked.

"A spring wedding would be perfect," Michelina added. "I could escort her back to America."

Spring! Tara's stomach turned.

"Absolutely not. I won't allow you to rush Tara. It's not fair to expect her to adapt to us and everything that comes with us so quickly," he told them, talking over their protests as he pulled Tara against him. "I refuse to jeopardize this marriage for the sake of speed."

The queen immediately turned silent. She gave a quick regal sigh of discontent, but inclined her head. "As you wish." She turned to Tara and took her hand. "Welcome to our family," she said gravely.

Guilt wiggled through her like a poisonous snake. Tara swallowed the bitter taste in her mouth. "Thank you, Your Majesty."

Michelina stepped forward and hugged her. "Welcome to the Dumonts. You will be my new sister."

More guilt. Tara forced herself to smile. "You're so kind."

Maggie pushed forward and hugged Nicholas first, then Tara. "You almost had me fooled this morning," she scolded playfully. "If you need an American ear for anything, you always have mine."

Then Michel welcomed her into the family with equal warmth, and Tara had to bite her tongue to keep from saying, *Just kidding. Hell will freeze over before Nicholas and I get married.*

Nicholas must have sensed that she was on the edge. "This is nice, but I'd like a few moments alone with my fiancée. I'm taking her for a walk in the garden," he said, reaching for her hand and leading her down the marble hallway. He swept her out a side door into the moonlit night, and Tara gulped deep breaths of the tropical air.

"I already don't like this," she told him. "You shouldn't have forced the proposal."

"I got rid of number seven, didn't I?" he returned with a trace of smugness.

She waved her hand. "Dickie was just desperate because my father didn't come through on the merger."

Nicholas shot her a look of doubt. "The man traveled around the world to get to you."

"To try to get to my father," Tara corrected.

"I don't think so. I think he wanted you."

Tara gaped at him. "You're insane. Totally insane. Is that the reason you pushed the engagement? Because you actually thought Dickie was operating under some misguided passion for me? You must have forgotten that I wrote the book on being resistible.''

"In light of the fact that *Dickie* traveled around the world to see you, you might need to do some revisions on your book," he said, loosening his tie and pacing along the garden path. "If he's known you since you were in kindergarten, then he probably knows you have killer legs under those ugly dresses and that your eyes talk when you don't. If he has a millimeter of testosterone, he's curious what you would be like in bed."

Tara's head began to spin. "Dickie probably doesn't even know what color my eyes are. He kissed me one time, and I made sure it was boring."

Nicholas wheeled around and faced her with a dangerous glint in his gaze. "Well, I know your eyes are blue, and your mouth is anything but boring."

Tara's heart stopped. A trickle of sexual excitement burned through her, quickly followed by confusion. "This is weird. We aren't supposed to be attracted to each other, remember?"

Shaking his head, he walked toward her. "I never said I wasn't attracted to you."

Tara's breath hitched as he loomed over her. "But we don't want to get married."

"Exactly," he said. "That's part of the attraction."

She blinked, the meaning of his words slogging through her brain at the speed of snails.

As if sensing her confusion, he elaborated. "You don't want to tell me what to do. I don't want to tell you what to do. Neither of us wants the ties that bind, but that doesn't mean I wouldn't mind having you in my bed.''

The following morning, Tara checked the results of her exam. Ninety-eight percent. Relief and exhilaration filled her chest to bursting. It was just a number, but it gave Tara hope. Hope that she wasn't nearly as useless as she'd feared. Hope that she could live on her own and find a way to contribute to the world. She still wasn't exactly sure how she could do that. She knew she just wanted to, badly.

And she would, she told herself with grim determination. She heard a knock at the door and her heart skipped. *For no good reason.* Nicholas. The man was full of contradictions. It had taken her half the night to settle down after he'd told her he wanted her in bed. Her stomach fluttered at the thought. She brushed her hand over her forehead and took a mind-clearing breath.

An outing with Nicholas. ''Heaven help me,'' she muttered at the sound of a second knock.

She turned off her computer and slowly walked toward the door. Tara wondered why she had a strange sense of foreboding about this outing. ''Lack of sleep,'' she said and opened the door.

Nicholas stood before her wearing a cap pulled low over his forehead, a pair of sunglasses, a casual white cotton shirt and a pair of casual slacks and tennis shoes.

No royal paraphernalia in sight. On closer inspection, she saw a stethoscope sticking out of his pants pocket.

She met his gaze. "So you're going to play doctor today?"

He gave a slight cringe. "You'll see soon enough. Fred will drive us, and we'll be riding on some dirt roads. You sure you don't get motion sickness?"

"I don't ride roller coasters, but I don't get motion sickness from a car ride," she said, growing curious despite her wariness about him.

He lifted an eyebrow above the sunglasses and nodded. "Then let's go," he said, and took her by the hand.

Ninety minutes later, as Fred drove the Jeep up a steep, narrow road, Tara bent forward to grab the purse she'd dropped on the vehicle's floor and felt her equilibrium spin. A kaleidoscope of colors and textures swam before her eyes. Green trees and splashes of pink flowers ran together. She sighed, wishing the dizzy feeling would go away. Forever.

They finally drew to a stop in front of an old wooden one-story building where a line of people wound down the street. "This would be easier if you stayed in the car, Fred," Nicholas said. "You just don't look geeky enough to be a med student."

Tara glanced at the huge, muscular bodyguard. He looked exactly like what he was—professional security.

"I can sit in the corner of the room and I'll be as quiet as a mouse," Fred said. "But I go where you go."

Nicholas sighed. "Okay, go do your security thing while Tara and I wait."

Fred nodded, and left the vehicle. Tara met Nicholas's gaze. "Will the other medical personnel in the clinic know your true identity?"

Nicholas nodded. "It's a two-edged sword. If doctors know I'm willing to donate my time, then they're more willing to donate theirs. I'm generally assigned young children or the elderly, because the youngsters don't recognize me and the elderly want to be heard and treated. They're not so picky about the doctor who treats them as long as he shows respect and listens."

"Why do you do this? Wouldn't it be easier to take a medical consultant job with the government?"

"You sound like my brother, Michel. He's committed to the government. I'm committed to the patient." He glanced out the window. "There's Fred. If anyone asks, you're a medical records assistant."

"What shall I call you?"

He cracked a grin that made her heart stutter. "Doctor," he said. "Doctor Do."

Fred opened the car door and the three of them walked into the small building temporarily operating as a community clinic. A nurse was waiting for Nicholas as soon as he walked past the cramped receiving area full of patients waiting to be seen. The nurse offered him a file and appeared to fight the urge to curtsey. "Dr. Do-Your-High—"

Nicholas shook his head. "Dr. Do," he said firmly. She nodded. "Three-year-old in number two, Doctor,'' she said, nodding toward the area divided by curtains. ''Fever and runny nose.''

Nicholas pulled off his sunglasses and motioned for Tara to follow. As she hurried after him, she couldn't help noticing the sense of purpose amidst the flurry of activity. She tripped over the uneven entrance into the partitioned area and barely managed to catch herself. Nicholas whipped around to steady her, his gaze meeting hers. ''Okay?'' he said, and his intensity made her feel as if the room was turning.

She nodded and carefully backed away. ''Okay.'' She glanced at the small child sitting on his mother's lap. ''Customer's waiting,'' she whispered.

For the next few minutes, she watched him perform a routine evaluation. Nicholas checked the child's pulse and throat, then listened to his chest and heart. Tara, however, caught the not-so-routine things Nicholas did that put the little boy at ease. She noticed that he talked to the child in a low, comforting voice and that his hands were gentle, yet firm.

It was clear that Nicholas was meant to be a physician. More than ever, she understood his single-minded intensity about his profession. Even in this brief instance with the three-year-old with an earache, Nicholas was making a difference, and she instinctively knew he was destined to make a huge difference in the lives of the people of Marceau. Watching him affected her in a strange way. She felt an odd, tight sensation in her chest and stomach.

Nicholas allowed the little boy to hold his stethoscope while he checked his ears. The little tike started to wail when Nicholas moved the tool for better viewing.

Nicholas nodded in sympathy. "You answered my question, big guy. Red and inflamed. All kinds of fluid in there." He wrote a prescription and passed it to Tara. "Get the people at the desk to fill this, along with providing some vitamins, while I talk to big guy's mom about his vaccinations."

It was a simple assignment. A child could have performed it, but Tara felt something she'd rarely felt during her entire life. Useful.

After that, she didn't seem to have time to stop. She was either collecting patient histories, fetching medication or vitamins or watching Nicholas as he examined patients and diagnosed illnesses.

At the end of the day nearly all of the other personnel had left when an elderly woman suffering from heat exhaustion was brought in. Delirious and pale, she batted away all attempts to give her water to drink or an IV, as she insisted she needed to find her children. Since any children she had would be middle-aged by now, she was clearly delusional. No one knew her name, her clothes were soiled and she looked as if she'd been wandering around for days. The woman wouldn't even allow Nicholas to examine her.

"We'll need to restrain her if she doesn't cooperate," Nicholas said.

The remaining lab technician and receptionist nodded in agreement. Fred stepped forward.

"Can I try to persuade her?" Tara asked impulsively, moved by the fear in the woman's eyes.

Nicholas glanced at her in surprise. "Okay, but we need to get some liquids into her immediately."

"Okay," Tara said, and filled three glasses with water, then closed the curtains in the room where the woman was pacing. Having reduced the light and insulated the patient from distraction, Tara sat down and took a sip from one of the glasses of water. "How many children do you have?" she addressed the woman.

The woman looked at Tara and frowned for a long moment. "Four," she said. "They're waiting at home for me to fix their dinner."

Tara nodded and patted the chair beside her. "You should leave soon, but it's very hot outside, isn't it? If you drink some water, maybe you won't get so hot when you go home."

The woman frowned at her again, but slowly sank into the chair beside her. Tara drew in a half breath of relief. One step at a time. She took another sip of water and offered one of the glasses to the woman.

"Do you have boys or girls?" Tara asked.

The woman took a drink of water. "Two boys, two girls. They keep me very busy."

Tara smiled and lifted her glass to her lips again. "I'm sure they do. If you're not feeding them or bathing them, I bet you're entertaining them."

"All the time," the woman said, taking several swallows of her own water. "My Henri can't stay out of the dirt."

Tara continued to talk and the woman continued to drink the water. As if her frantic energy drained from her, the woman grew drowsy. "I feel very tired."

"You look like you don't feel very well. Would you let the doctor examine you?" Tara asked.

The woman nodded and closed her eyes.

Nicholas immediately went to her side and took her pulse. In the course of listening to her heart, he lifted a necklace from beneath her blouse with a health alert medallion.

"Diabetes," he said. "Tell the med tech I need insulin and a saline IV."

Nicholas worked on the woman for several hours, stabilizing her until they could move her to the nearest residential clinic one hour away. The glazed look in the woman's eyes faded, and she was finally able to recall her name. Her frantic relatives were contacted and planned to visit her early the following morning.

Leaving the residential clinic, Tara didn't know what time it was as she stumbled over a stone and pitched forward to her knees. Pain shot through her. Gasping for breath, she felt Nicholas's arm wrap around her waist and pull her upright against him.

"Okay?" he asked, his deep voice sending a shiver down the back of her neck.

Tara tried to squeeze a smidgen of oxygen into her deprived lungs and brain. She nodded, drowning in a combination of embarrassment and hyperawareness of Nicholas's hard body at her back.

"Are you sure?" he asked, turning her in his arms. "Are you breathing yet?"

I would if you would stop touching me, she thought. Tara deliberately inhaled a deep breath of air. "Breathing," she said with a nervous smile. "See? I'm fine. The ground moved when I wasn't looking."

He frowned and glanced down at her legs. "Any scrapes?"

"I'm fine. Just tired and a little embarrassed," she insisted. "Could we please go back to the palace now?"

He glanced at his watch and nodded. "Of course. The queen will have my head for keeping you out so late. And if she knew I'd put you to work in a free health clinic—" He broke off and shook his head.

"I liked it," Tara said, still integrating everything she'd experienced today. She felt bone-tired but satisfied. In fact, she couldn't remember feeling this satisfied in her life. "Do you go every day?" she asked as Fred held open the door to the Jeep.

Before replying Nicholas murmured a thanks to the bodyguard, then climbed in beside Tara. Fred drove the vehicle down the winding mountain road. "Not every day. I have state and family functions I'm required to attend. I'd love to have my own practice, but this is the next best thing. The more often I work at the free clinics, the more effective I am when I ask other physicians to donate some of their time. Someday I may accept a more official position with the government, but I'll always want to practice medicine with actual patients."

"And you should," she said, remembering how effective and caring he'd been with his patients in the clinic today.

Curiosity flashed across his face. "I should what?"

Tara heard just a tinge of the royal surprise in his voice that she would dare tell him he "should" do anything. She smiled. "You should always practice medicine directly with people because you're very good."

He looked at her for a long moment, then gave a short, humorless chuckle. "I haven't heard that from anyone in my family."

"They obviously haven't seen you in action."

Pleasure crossed his face, and he held her gaze. "Speaking of action...how did you know what to do with Celia?"

Celia was the mother of four who'd been suffering from dehydration. Tara shook her head and shrugged. "Lucky guess. Instinct. Believe me, it was nothing I'd read. I just thought maybe we'd make a little more progress if we stopped fighting her and went along with her instead. She was so concerned about her children. I thought maybe if she talked about them, she might unwind a little bit."

He lifted his hand to push back a strand of her hair. "And you were right," he said, studying her as if she were a surprise to him. "You didn't complain about helping, either."

"It was fun," she told him, trying to remain unaffected by the sensual sensation of his fingers in her hair. "I'd like to go again sometime."

"Really?" he asked, his eyes widening in surprise.

"Really," she said.

"That could be arranged."

"I'd like that."

"In the meantime, we're stopping for a swim. Fred," he said to the driver, "pull over at Augustus Beach."

"A swim?" Alarm kicked through Tara. "But it's midnight."

He shrugged. "Not a problem. This is a private beach for the family."

"But I didn't bring a suit."

Nicholas chuckled, and Tara saw a dangerously devilish glint in his eyes. "Neither did I."

Seven

Nicholas ducked his head under the cool ocean water to bring down his body temperature. Sitting close to Tara in the Jeep with no distractions aroused a mother lode of carnal instincts. He couldn't explain it. He didn't know if it was the look in her eyes or the way she bit her lip or her sweet and spicy scent. All he knew was that during the drive he was thinking about talking her out of her clothes and ravaging her.

She would be appalled if she knew he was fixated on the idea of sliding between her silky white thighs and pushing himself inside her until they both exploded.

Nicholas swallowed a groan and dunked himself under the water once more. He couldn't stay under too long, because he knew he was being watched by

Fred. Fred knew the queen was twitchy on the subject of swimming. It all went back to when Nicholas's youngest brother fell overboard all those years ago. If Queen Anna had her way, none of her children or grandchildren would ever go swimming.

Nicholas had long ago chafed at his mother's restraints, and his bodyguards had learned to watch without interfering. Nicholas glanced at the shore and a full moon illuminated Tara's profile along the shore.

He grinned to himself. She was curious, though she'd sworn she wouldn't leave the car, let alone get in the ocean with him.

"Come on in. The water's great," he coaxed, despite the fact that the water temperature was a little on the chilly side.

"It looks cold," she called back.

"It's great! I wouldn't have taken you for a water wuss," he yelled, deliberately goading her.

Even with the short distance between them, he saw her chin snap up. "I'm not," she retorted.

"Prove it."

"I don't have to prove anything to you."

True, he thought, and decided to move to shore.

He watched her kick off her shoes, and he stopped in midstroke. She began to unbutton her shirt, and his heart stood still.

"Turn around!" she yelled at him.

It cost him dearly, but he yielded, turning toward the dark horizon. He knew the minute she hit the water from her yelp of accusation.

"You lied. It's freezing!"

"Invigorating," he corrected with a chuckle. He stole a glimpse over his shoulder, but to his frustration she was already covered by the water.

"Cold," she said, swimming toward him.

Treading water, Nicholas turned around to face her. "You must admit it feels good after such a long day at the clinic."

"Bracing," she conceded, swimming beside him. "But more than few minutes in here and you'll have to treat me for hypothermia."

He reached for her hand and tugged. "Shared body heat is an excellent prevention against hypothermia."

"So is staying out of cold water," she shot back, reluctantly allowing him to draw her against him.

He felt the brush of her tight nipples against his chest and her bare belly against his. Her thighs brushed his, and the carnal thoughts he'd held back ran through his brain like wildfire. Tara's hair was slicked back and the apples of her cheeks were dotted with drops of water.

"You look like a mermaid," he said.

"I can't look like a mermaid," she replied, her gaze intently curious, but wary. "No fins."

"Your face, your hair, your eyes. You look like a siren from the sea."

She leaned closer and bit her lip, driving him a little crazy with the gesture. "Do you always say wacky things when you've worked a long day?" she whispered.

Nicholas grinned. "No. Just when I've worked a long day with a mermaid. Quit biting your lip."

She frowned, her breasts brushing against him in tantalizing torture once again. "Why?"

"So I can kiss you," he said, and lowered his head as her eyes widened. Her lips were soft and tasted faintly salty from the water. He rubbed his mouth over all of hers, sucking on her lips, rubbing his tongue over the seam. She opened her mouth ever so slightly in invitation, and he plunged inside to where she was warm, wet and welcoming. Even with the cool water surrounding him, he felt himself grow warm. And when her tongue twined with his, he felt himself grow hard under the water.

Nicholas felt the raging, ripping desire to consume her totally, starting with her lips and stopping with her... Hell, and not stopping.

He slid his hands over her back, pressing her bare breasts against his chest. Good, but he wanted more. He slid one hand down to her buttocks to wind her legs around him. The slim barrier of cotton she wore made him groan. "I want you naked," he muttered against her mouth.

Clinging to his shoulders, she pulled back slightly and looked at him with eyes full of arousal and confusion. "Things are moving too fast. What are we doing? I thought we were just supposed to be pretending to be engaged."

"We are," he assured her. "I told you that doesn't mean I don't want you."

She shook her head. "You could have anybody. Why me? Because I'm safe? Or because I'm convenient?"

Nicholas hadn't thought more deeply about this than appeasing the need she stirred in him so easily. He hadn't wanted to think any more deeply, but she was forcing him to. "The words 'safe' or 'convenient' don't come to mind," he said, and pulled her against him again. "I want you because you see me as a man. I want the honesty I see in your eyes. I want the passion underneath your skin. I can feel it." He slid his hand over her breast and toyed with her nipple.

She gasped, and he took her mouth again. This time, she opened quickly, matching the strokes of his tongue with her own. He squeezed her bottom and she undulated against him. If not for the scrap of cotton between them, he could be inside her. The thought nearly drove him mad.

He felt her start to shiver and realized the cold was getting to her. He lingered over her lips, then carried her toward the beach. Her wet, nearly naked body slid down his as she stood in front of him. Her breasts still pressed against him, taunting him.

"This feels more than a little crazy to me," she whispered.

"It will keep feeling crazy until we do something about it," he told her.

Her eyes darkened. "I'm not sure that what you have in mind is really a solution."

"Do you have an alternative suggestion?" he challenged.

"I don't know," she said, and with a deep breath pulled away from him. She'd better come up with something and soon, because she felt he was pulling her into a vast, sensual vortex…and part of her was eager to be drawn in even farther.

Tara's sleep was filled with disturbing, tantalizing images of Nicholas kissing her, making love to her. Bowing to her weariness, she slept late the following morning. A knock on the door woke her, and she jerked upward. Big mistake. The room felt as if it turned. Tara automatically tilted her head to one side and counted.

Nicholas burst through the door with a breakfast tray in his hands. "Good morning, sleepyhead. Did I wake you?"

Tara continued to count.

He frowned when she didn't respond. He set the tray down on her bedside table and bent over her. "What's wrong?"

"Just waiting for the room to" —she blinked and slowly met his gaze— "stop moving. It did. And yes, you woke me, but breakfast looks good." She eased into a sitting position.

Nicholas reached out and cradled her head in his hands. Her heart raced until she saw that he was gazing at her with a look of professional scrutiny in his eyes. "How often do you experience vertigo?" he asked.

"I don't know. I haven't paid that much attention. Sometimes I go for months without the dizziness. Then it seems like I get hit with it every other day." She shrugged. "I'm sure it's nothing serious. Just a little equilibrium problem I've had since I was eleven.''

"Do you notice if it's brought on by sudden movements?''

Tara thought about the times she had lost her balance. "Maybe. I haven't paid that much attention to how I feel before I fall, because I'm usually spending more energy putting on Band-Aids afterward,'' she said wryly. "Why do you ask?''

"Because I'm taking you to visit a friend of mine,'' Nicholas said, still studying her eyes.

"When and where?'' she asked, plucking his fingers from her head. Nicholas might be able to endure such close proximity to her without becoming rattled, but she couldn't say the same. She reached for a croissant from the breakfast tray and took a bite.

"Today. Paris.''

Tara nearly choked on her roll. "Paris? Why?''

"He's a medical specialist. I want him to examine you.''

Tara felt an odd mixture of hope and fear. Although her clumsiness had been the bane of her existence, she'd always assumed her problem was just that— terminal but simple clumsiness. What if there was a medical reason for her lack of coordination? What if it could be fixed? "Do you really think there's something wrong with me? Something medical?''

"Maybe. There are a lot of things you don't do because you don't want to fall. I think you owe it to yourself to find out.''

Excitement rushed through her, and she threw back the covers of her bed. "When can we go?"

Nicholas chuckled. "I think you might want to get dressed."

Just two hours later, the royal jet carrying Nicholas and Tara landed in Paris, and they were whisked into a limousine which carried them through the busy streets to an office on the West Bank where Nicholas's associate, Dr. Antoine Bordeau, greeted both of them. Tara filled out an extensive questionnaire, then answered even more questions from the kindly but persistent Dr. Bordeau. After a thorough physical examination and lab work, he shook his head and muttered to himself in French.

"Tell me it's nothing serious," Tara said, curious to know if the doctor had learned anything or if the trip had been a wild-goose chase.

Dr. Bordeau smiled and shook his head. "'Serious' is a relative term. I believe your vertigo may be related to an inner ear problem."

"But don't people with inner ear problems usually get nauseous?"

"Often, but not always. I think you have learned to compensate for this problem over the years. Crystals form, and if they are displaced in the semicircular balance canals, they can stimulate the balance nerve inappropriately. From my examination, I believe it is your right ear. And you said you tend to fall toward your right? Yes?"

"Yes," she murmured, not knowing whether to be

relieved or dismayed that there was a physical reason for her lack of coordination.

"This is a very satisfying kind of condition to treat because the treatment is a repositioning procedure and it's ninety-five percent effective."

"You mean I might not be a klutz anymore after today?" she asked, amazed at the prospect.

"Let's see what happens," he said.

Forty-five minutes later, Tara walked out of the doctor's office with follow-up instructions for the next forty-eight hours. "That was too easy," Tara said, almost afraid to hope Dr. Bordeau had been right. "Too easy."

"Just follow Dr. Bordeau's instructions, and you should notice a difference pretty soon," Nicholas said.

"But why didn't my doctor back in the States catch this?" asked Tara, confused and a little angry, as Nicholas escorted her to the limo.

"I think it's like you said. Your doctor was usually focused on trying to repair the damage caused by the vertigo, and you're not much of a complainer."

She shot him a dark look. "Are you saying I should have been more of a whiner?"

Nicholas paused, then nodded. "Yes. If something was bothering you, if you felt dizzy, then you should have told someone."

"My father was already so disappointed in me, I didn't want to emphasize my shortcomings any more by complaining. I know he would have much preferred having a boy instead of a girl, especially after my mother died when I was seven." Tara felt a slice of pain mingled with embarrassment at what she'd revealed. She'd always known she didn't measure up to what her father had expected from her.

Nicholas gently tapped his finger on her nose. "You've gotten awfully quiet. What's the American expression? A penny for your thoughts?"

She gave a sad smile. "I think this is one of those times when I could pay a professional a lot of pennies to talk about my thoughts. I could hold a pity party about how much I wanted to please my father but couldn't. I was raised in luxury and given a fine private school education. I've never been hungry except by choice, and I have received material gifts other people could only dream of. I would be an ungrateful wretch to complain."

Nicholas looked into Tara's eyes and caught a glimpse of something rarer than diamonds—a pure heart. He took her hand. He understood exactly what Tara was saying because he too had been provided with every possible material gift. Unlike Tara, however, Nicholas had also been given the gift of family, and from his brother Michel, he'd received unwavering belief and support. If ever anyone deserved the same, it was Tara. He took her small hands in his. It bothered the hell out of him that she had missed so much, that she had hurt so much. "You're an interesting woman. You remind me of everything good I want to be."

She shook her head, and her eyes grew shiny with unshed tears. "I can't imagine how I do that, but if

Dr. Bordeau's treatment works, my life will be totally changed. And it will be because of you.''

Nicholas got a kick out of the expectant joy in her eyes. "After your forty-eight hours is up, what's the first thing you want to do?"

Her eyes widened. "Oh, ten things all at once. Dance, run, skip.'' Her face lit up like a Christmas tree. "Drive a car."

For Tara, the forty-eight hours passed at an excruciatingly slow pace. She followed Dr. Bordeau's instructions to the letter, and urged Nicholas to go visit the clinics. She slept upright and avoided any quick jarring movements. Five minutes before the end of her vigil, a knock sounded on her door.

Certain it was Nicholas, she opened the door. "I have five more minutes," she said, and laughed nervously. She was so relieved to see him her hands trembled. She laced them together.

"Let's check for nystagmus," Nicholas said, and she would swear he was almost as eager as she was.

"What's that?" she asked.

"Involuntary eye movements triggered by inner ear stimulation," he said, and performed a short examination similar to one Dr. Bordeau had performed.

He finished and met her gaze. "Put on your dancing shoes. I'll pick you up at eight o'clock tonight."

He gave her a quick kiss, then left her staring after him. It took a full moment before Tara realized the procedure had worked. She let out a whoop of joy and pinched herself. Her mind reeled with possibilities. Independence was possible for her now. Indeed, it was so close, she could practically taste it.

Moments later, another knock sounded on her door. Tara opened it to find Maggie staring at her with a worried but expectant expression. "Is everything okay?"

Michel's wife must have heard her shriek of joy. Barely able to contain her happiness, Tara bounced on her toes. "Everything is more than wonderful. I'm not going to be a klutz anymore! I've been cured."

Maggie's brow wrinkled in confusion. "Cured?" she echoed.

Tara told Maggie the long, somewhat sad story about her lack of coordination and vertigo and how Nicholas had taken her to Dr. Bordeau.

Maggie's eyes gleamed with approval. "What a story. So Nicholas is taking you dancing tonight. What are you going to wear?"

Tara thought about her wardrobe, and some of the air went out of her balloon. She made a face and looked into the closet. "Oh, good point. I only brought uglywear." She glanced at the clock. "Do you think some shops might still be open?"

Maggie nodded. "Yes, but this isn't my area of expertise."

"Michelina? Do you really think she'd want to go shopping with me?"

Maggie rolled her eyes. "Do fish swim?"

Within no time, Michelina made arrangements with four dress shops and two shoe stores, and she and

Tara were riding toward town in the armored Mercedes.

"The armor is overkill, but Mother won't allow me out without it," Michelina said with a long-suffering expression.

"Only daughter," Tara said. "You must be so important to her."

"She's protecting her investment. She's hoping I'll draw in a marriage partner who will do great things for Marceau."

"Surely there's more to it than that," Tara said. "I'm sure royal duty is always a given, and I know I'm an outsider looking in, but it appears that Queen Anna is very proud and protective of all of you."

"Yes," Michelina admitted. "But she's way too protective. You probably wouldn't understand, since you're planning to marry my brother, but I want nothing more than to be independent."

Tara felt a slice of guilt at her deception. She bit her lip. "I understand wanting to make your own decisions, wanting to find your own way instead of following someone else's direction," she said quietly.

Michelina tilted her well-coifed head, giving Tara an assessing glance. "My brother Nicholas has always had a talent for looking beneath the surface. From the beginning, Tara, he said there was more to you than what met the eye. You're different from the usual woman my mother parades in front of him." She smiled. "You must be very special for him to be so determined to marry you."

It was all Tara could do not to correct Michelina.

All she could do to keep from saying that what she and Nicholas shared was a deep, passionate desire *not* to get married. She opened her mouth, then closed it. "You're definitely right about me being different from his other marital prospects," she said as the limo drew to a stop in front of a boutique. "I bet I win the award for the ugliest clothing."

Michelina's eyes widened as if she were surprised that Tara was aware of how unattractive her clothes were. She patted her hand. "We're about to change that—and more."

"And more?" Tara echoed, unable to keep a note of distress from creeping into her voice.

"Not to worry. You're in good hands."

Three hours later, Tara and Michelina returned to the palace with three new outfits, matching shoes, and foundation garments so skimpy, merely thinking about them brought a blush to Tara's cheek. And just when Tara thought Michelina was done with her high-octane fashion makeover, Nicholas's sister led Tara to the palace salon, where a stylist awaited her.

Tara drew the line at a bikini wax, but Henri cut and styled her hair, then applied makeup.

Delighted with the result, Michelina threw her arms around Tara. "*Belle, belle!* I can't wait to see Nicholas's face when he sees you. He'll have to pick his jaw up off the floor."

"I don't know how to thank you," Tara said, catching a glimpse of her reflection in the mirror and barely recognizing herself. Part of her craved the safety of her pre-makeover self. That Tara wouldn't turn heads. This one… Well, she supposed she would find out if this version would turn Nicholas's head. Her stomach dipped at the thought.

"Oh, this was all my pleasure," Michelina said. "Believe me, you've saved me from another interminably boring day in the castle keep. Now go get dressed. I want to see the complete effect."

It didn't take Tara long to dress. She glanced at the mirror every now and then, but the image of herself combined with the prospect of dancing with Nicholas unsettled her more than words. Michelina raved over the transformation.

Eight o'clock arrived, but Nicholas didn't. Another hour passed and Michelina was steaming. "Medicine is like a mistress to Nicholas," she muttered, growing more offended by the moment. In fact, Tara thought Nicholas's sister was more offended than she herself was. Tara felt a strange combination of disappointment and relief.

Nicholas's sister was determined that all her hard work not go to waste.

"Well, there's no other solution," Michelina declared at last. You and I will go to the disco without him."

Eight

Tara wasn't exactly sure how she'd ended up in Marceau's loudest, most crowded disco dancing with two men at one time, but Michelina had a heck of a lot to do with it. Nicholas's sister had mowed Tara's protests flat to the ground, insisting that both Tara and Nicholas needed to learn a lesson from this situation. Nicholas needed to learn that Tara wasn't always going to sit at home waiting for him, and Tara needed to learn to entertain herself in his absence.

Under the watchful eye of two palace security men, Tara and Michelina gyrated to an old American disco tune rerecorded in French. One song blended into another, and Tara reveled in her newfound balance.

When the deejay put on a slow song, she thought she would take a break, but her dance partners thought differently.

Nicholas walked into the disco and worked at tamping down the odd tension he felt in his gut. When he'd arrived at the palace to learn that Michelina had taken Tara for a girls' night out, he'd immediately smelled trouble. Michelina had a zest for life and excitement that was fast turning his mother's hair gray. Tara was probably stuck in a corner of the disco longing for quiet.

Surveying the crowd, he easily spotted Michelina, but not Tara. Fred pointed to a woman with long brown hair who wore a black dress that revealed shapely legs and a curvy body. He noticed that the foreign minister's son was wrapped around her like an octopus.

Nicholas blinked and shook his head. Not Tara. The woman turned her head and he saw the shape of her cheek and her full mouth. His temperature shot through the roof.

Striding through the crowd, he tapped the foreign minister's son on the shoulder and in French curtly informed the young man that he was cutting in.

Tara's eyes lit up. "Nicholas."

Nicholas looked appraisingly at her before he pulled her into his arms. "I see my sister's handiwork," he said tightly.

"She's amazing, isn't she?"

"Yes, amazing. I apologize for being so late. There

was an emergency," he said, confused as hell by his possessive feelings.

Tara shrugged. "That's what I figured. I was all set to go to bed, but Michelina insisted I needed to learn to entertain myself if I was going to be married to a doctor." Tara rolled her eyes and lowered her voice. "I really hate deceiving your family."

Nicholas saw the tinge of guilt in her eyes, but his mind was fixated on the idea of Tara entertaining herself. "I see you met Roberto," he said.

"Michelina introduced me. He's been very kind to dance with me tonight," she said. "I'm such an amateur."

Nicholas bit back an oath. "I don't think 'kind' is the accurate word, considering he was wrapped around you so tightly I wondered if we would need the jaws of life to separate you."

Tara pulled back and looked at him. "You don't think he was really interested in me that way, do you?"

He felt his skin prickle with frustration. "Tara, with the way you look tonight, any man with a drop of testosterone would want to take you to bed."

She blinked at him as if it took a moment for her to digest his statement. Sensual awareness darkened her eyes to almost black. "Does that include you?"

Nicholas felt himself turn rock hard with arousal. He'd tried every trick in the book to deny it and push it aside by working, but he was tired, edgy and hungry. Sexually hungry. And unlike every other man in the room, he knew what was beneath Tara's fitted dress.

He'd lost any inclination to be sensible when he'd walked into the disco and found Tara in another man's arms. He drew her lower body against his and looked deeply into her eyes. "You sound curious."

She swallowed, but didn't move away from him. "I guess I am."

"I can answer all your questions," he said, guiding her to the side of the room. He knew they were being watched. Instinct, long drummed into him, reminded him to take care. Another part of him didn't give a damn.

She tentatively undulated against him in rhythm with the music. Nicholas had a completely carnal urge to rip off her clothes. Instead, he lowered his hands to her hips and nudged her chin up to kiss her.

She welcomed his tongue, sucking him deep into her mouth while he rocked between her thighs. Each stroke of her tongue, each movement of her pelvis against his, was like a double intimate stroke. His heart hammered in his chest and his skin turned hot.

Guiding her farther into the darkness of the room, he lowered his hand to the hem of her skirt and rubbed his fingers over her bare, silky skin. He couldn't resist the urge to skim his hand up her leg. When he learned by touch that she was wearing a thong, he nearly burst the front of his slacks.

"I have to take you out of here," he told her. "I need to be alone with you."

Nicholas swept Tara from the disco to a waiting limo. ''No Jeep?'' she said in surprise.

''The Mercedes affords more privacy,'' he replied, and his gaze scored her with heat.

From the minute she had seen Nicholas, Tara's heart had beat double time, and it showed no sign of slowing down. Her body felt flushed inside and out from the way he looked at her and touched her. She knew everything between them was about to change, and she couldn't find the power in herself to stop it.

Wisdom and restraint scattered to the wind with the sweeping force of a hurricane. Raging need, which she read on Nicholas's face and felt reverberating inside herself, wouldn't be denied.

As soon as he followed her into the car, Nicholas pushed a button, and the privacy window rose between the driver and the back seat. Nicholas immediately took her mouth in a kiss that left her breathless.

Tara felt herself sinking into a deep, warm pool of arousal where instinct ruled over inhibition. Nicholas devoured her mouth, and she drew his tongue into her mouth. He slid his hands over her body as if to learn every curve and indentation. He moved one hand up her rib cage with agonizing slowness to the underside of her breasts. Her nipple pebbled against the lace bra, and she shifted restlessly. Tara yearned for a full touch.

''What do you want?'' he asked, his voice smooth with sexual taunting. ''This?'' He closed his hand over her breast and she couldn't hold back a sound of satisfaction.

He groaned at the sound as if she were torturing him. He slid his hand under the hem of her dress between her thighs. He found the elastic band of her panties and rubbed his thumb on the soft sensitive skin underneath. Tara held her breath while a rush of expectancy roared through her. She shifted to allow him freer access and he began to swear.

"Damn it! I don't want to wait until we get back to the palace." He looked deep into her eyes with a gaze that rocked her to her core, then took her mouth in a carnal kiss.

Tara had the sense that she had been waiting for this moment her entire life. Nicholas pulled his head away, and his nostrils flared as he pushed the intercom button. "Take the long way home," he ordered to the driver.

Nicholas turned off the intercom, then returned his undivided attention to Tara. "This dress has annoyed me since the moment I saw you in it," he said, moving his hands to the back of her dress.

Surprise shot through her. "You don't like it?"

"I like it so much that I want it off," he said, and lowered the zipper in one slow, competent movement.

Her breath stopped.

He didn't.

He pushed the dress down to her waist, drinking in the sight of her bare torso and lace-covered breasts. Without pausing a beat, he unhooked her bra and bared her breasts. His eyelids heavy with sensual approval, he lifted his thumbs to her nipples, and the delicious sensation teased them to tight buds.

Tara felt the wanting inside her tighten. She arched toward Nicholas and he acknowledged her feminine invitation. Lowering his head, he drew a nipple into his mouth. She felt a corresponding tension in her lower regions. Unable to stop herself, she arched again and he groaned. The sound vibrated over her flesh, sending her nerve endings into a frenzy.

Turning his attention to her other nipple, he swirled his tongue around her until she began to squirm with pleasure.

"Good, *ma chérie?*" he muttered. "I'm just getting started."

He pushed her dress the rest of the way down her hips so that she was completely naked with the exception of the black satin thong and strappy black sandals.

She felt another rush of heat and desire rise to her head, making her vision hazy with arousal. Tara had never felt so many sensations at once. She tugged at Nicholas's shirt, eager to feel his naked skin against hers. His flesh burned with the same heat that throbbed inside her. She ran her hands over his chest and lower to his abdomen.

He sucked in a quick breath and narrowed his eyes. "Go on," he said, with a combination of challenge and need.

With trembling hands, Tara unfastened his slacks and eased the zipper down over the bulge of his masculinity. She slid her hands beneath his briefs to touch him intimately, to caress him.

He let out a long hiss of a sigh at her touch, then stilled her hand with his. "Later," he said, lowering his head to drop openmouthed kisses down her abdomen. He removed her little thong and pushed her legs apart to kiss her at the top of her thighs.

Tara stiffened at the shocking intimacy, but Nicholas was clearly determined. Reassuringly he caressed her thighs while he mesmerized her with his magic tongue in her most sensitive, secret feminine place.

With each delicious stroke against her femininity, she felt the tension inside her tighten like a bow. He drew her into his mouth as if to consume her, and the sensation was too much. She tumbled over the edge, calling out his name and free-falling into his arms.

With a combination of possessive satisfaction and unspent need stamped on his face, Nicholas shed his slacks and underwear and rose over her with purpose. He put on a condom and lifted her limp arms so that she clasped his shoulders. "Hold on," he told her and thrust inside her.

The overstretched sensation took her breath.

Nicholas looked at her in surprise and turned perfectly, rigidly still inside her. "You should have told me," he muttered.

Tara licked her dry lips and inhaled a shallow breath of air. "I, uh, my brain—" She broke off and shook her head, unable to form a complete thought except that she didn't want him to stop. "Don't stop," she whispered.

Something primitive flickered in his light blue eyes and he began to move in a slow rhythm that muddied her mind all over again. He filled her completely. In her mind, body and soul, there was only Nicholas, taking and giving, making her want to give him everything.

His breath grew short, his movements swift and his body gleamed with the promise of satisfaction. She saw the moment he climaxed, the pleasure in his eyes. She was filled with the heady knowledge that she had helped put that expression in his gaze, and Tara had never felt more complete.

Moments passed in which the only sound in the limo was their combined breaths. Then Nicholas rose slightly and brushed his lips over Tara's cheek. He pulled away, switching positions so that she lay on top of him.

Tara's heart was doing strange things. She felt glorious, but vulnerable. "I have a question," she finally managed. "Was this supposed to make our situation less crazy?"

Nicholas chuckled, looping his hand around the back of her neck and drawing her lips against his. "You're a psychology major. You should know that repression is bad for your mental health."

All too conscious of his muscular body beneath hers, Tara tried to rein in her brain. "Yes, but I don't feel less crazy. I mean, if making love with you once was supposed to clear my mind, then—"

"Once!" Nicholas said, looking at her as if she'd

lost her mind. "What made you think we were just going to make love once?"

"Well, if we made a habit of it when we're trying to convince everyone that we're going to get married when we're not going to get married, then—" She broke off in confusion. "Wouldn't that be just too weird?"

He shook his head. "No. It just means we have an understanding."

"Oh," Tara said, still confused. She made a face and tried to draw away from him in hopes that she could then think more clearly, but Nicholas tightened his arms around her. "Would you mind explaining this understanding?"

He met her gaze. "We understand each other. You understand that medicine is the most important thing to me and I understand that you getting your education is the most important thing to you. We are extremely attracted to each other," he said, skimming his hand down her arm. "But we don't want to get married. We will behave as if we're engaged because it suits our individual goals."

Tara felt a rush of conflicting emotions. "What if something goes wrong?"

"What could go wrong?"

"What if we fall in love with each other?"

Nicholas shook his head and smiled. "Won't happen. We're both too focused. That's the beauty of it." He gently squeezed her derriere and rose to a sitting position with her in his lap. "It's a damn shame, but you need to get dressed so we can go back to the palace. We can have a midnight snack in my quarters, and you can stay with me.''

With his gaze hungry for her and his arms wrapped around her, it was hard for Tara to give voice to the little whispers of doubt in the back of her mind. Her options were staying with Nicholas or staying by herself. Her heart offered no choice in the matter. Trying to get a handle on the euphoria racing through her veins like a drug, she got dressed.

Her legs were unsteady as she walked with Nicholas into the palace, but her shaky balance had nothing to do with her inner ear problem. The man had blown her away, yet he seemed totally at ease, laughing and teasing her.

As promised, they ate a midnight snack of sandwiches and soda. Nicholas told her about the medical emergency that had made him late.

''I delivered a baby,'' he told her casually.

Tara felt a pang of disappointment. ''What a bummer!''

''Bummer?'' he said, clearly perplexed.

''I would have loved to have been there,'' she said. ''Was it fun?''

He smiled and drew her close to him on his big bed. ''Yeah.'' He shook his head. ''Not every woman would be so interested in what I do.''

''But what you do is fascinating. You make a big difference in a lot of people's lives. I wish I could do the same,'' she added wistfully.

He toyed with her hair thoughtfully. ''You may underestimate your impact.''

She shot him a skeptical look. "Nice of you to say, but I think not. One day, though, I will make a difference, some sort of contribution. It may not be as dramatic as what you do, but I'll find a way to do something."

"I'm sure you will," he said, his gaze sliding over her like a hot fire. "In the meantime, I can make a suggestion for how you can contribute," he said, taking her mouth in a kiss that made her head fuzzy all over again. "To me."

The following morning, Nicholas awakened to a glorious sunrise and the even more glorious sight of Tara, naked, in his bed. Impossible though it seemed, he felt himself grow hard with wanting. His response was disconcerting as hell considering the fact that they had made love throughout the night. He wanted her again, but she was inexperienced, and he didn't want to make her sore.

Her eyes fluttered open. He watched confusion, followed by recognition, then self-consciousness, flit through her eyes. Wanting to wipe the self-consciousness away, he gave her a quick kiss.

"What in hell are you doing naked in my bed this morning?" he asked in a mock-serious tone.

She hesitated, then gave a tiny shake of her head. "You invited me to your bed." A smile tugged the corners of her lips upward like the morning sun rising on the horizon. "Then, when I politely tried not to overstay my welcome, you trapped me with your big, heavy leg."

His lips twitched. "I don't recall hearing any complaints. In fact, I could swear I heard you say something like 'Oh, Nicholas, don't stop. Oh, Nicholas, you feel so good. Oh, Nicholas—'"

Tara covered his mouth with her hand and tossed him a dark glance. "It's incredibly impolite of you to tease me this way."

He lowered his head, so that his nose rubbed hers. "You don't arouse my polite feelings."

"No, I obviously arouse your baser emotions," she said in a delicious breathless voice that made him reconsider giving her some time to recover from their wild night of lovemaking.

It cost him, but he exercised restraint. "Since I was late for our dance date last night, I'd like to make up for it today. I need to make a few phone calls, then you name whatever you want to do today."

She pulled back slightly, and her gaze dipped and swayed over his body with sensual secrets.

Nicholas groaned. "Except that. I don't want to make you sore. Stop looking at me like that."

"Like what?"

"Like a she-devil bent on ravaging my body," he said.

Her mouth dropped open. "I've never been called a she-devil."

"That's because no other man knows what you're capable of in bed," he retorted, and it occurred to him that he didn't like the idea of any other man finding out what Tara was like in bed. "Stop distracting me,'' he said. ''Tell me what you want to do today.''

She paused a half beat, then met his gaze with the force of an oncoming truck. ''I want you to teach me to drive.''

Oh, hell.

Nine

"Give it some gas. Let out the clutch," Nicholas said for what had to be the fiftieth time.

Not enough gas, too little clutch. The Jeep sputtered, choked and died. In the Mercedes parked a short distance away, Nicholas saw Fred lift the page of the newspaper he had rested on the steering wheel.

Tara sighed in deep discouragement. She thumped the steering wheel with her fist and frowned. "I thought I had left my lack of coordination behind with my inner ear problem."

"That doesn't mean you'll instantly know how to drive a vehicle with manual transmission. That requires technique and practice," Nicholas said, wondering if his teeth were loose or just felt that way.

"Human spark plugs would help," he muttered to himself.

"Pardon?" Tara said.

"Nothing. You know, you could start out with a vehicle with automatic transmission, and I bet you would be gliding down the highway in no time."

She pursed her mouth and shook her head. "No. It's got to be a Jeep. I want to be able to drive a Jeep when you let me go with you to another medical clinic."

Nicholas felt his heart squeeze tight in his chest at the earnest expression on Tara's face. "You don't have to drive, Tara. That's why I have Fred."

"But what if there's an emergency and he can't drive and you need to look after a patient? I should be able to drive a Jeep."

"I can't imagine that happening. Stop torturing yourself about learning to drive a Jeep, and let's kick Fred out of the Mercedes and take it for a spin."

Tara sighed again and looked out the window. "I don't want to be useless."

The pain in her voice sliced at him. He took her hand. "You're not useless."

"Oh, really? Then tell me all the useful things I've done since I arrived in Marceau," she challenged him.

Nicholas looked into her blue eyes full of doubt and hope and drew a blank. Biting back an oath, he raked his fingers through his hair. This was important, blast it. "Maggie told me you helped her and Max find Elvis."

"I whistled."

"It was useful. You appeared with me at the ball and kept me from getting nagged to death by my mother."

"I stepped on your foot," she reminded him.

"A technicality," he said. "You temporarily kept the peace between Michelina and the queen with your diplomacy."

"*Temporarily* is the operative word there. Those two are headed for World War Three."

He couldn't disagree. "You coaxed a delirious woman into accepting medical treatment. And you made me feel good about what I'm doing with the free medical clinics when everyone else at the palace would like me to do something else."

Tara was silent for a long moment. "I think you would have found a way to treat Cecile, and I know nothing will prevent you from practicing medicine. Nothing should."

Nicholas couldn't argue her point. How could he make her see that she was important, that she made things easier just by her presence?

"Let me try again," she said, putting the Jeep into neutral. "If I can get out of neutral three times without stalling, I'll take that as success."

It took the rest of the afternoon, but Tara finally succeeded. As soon as they returned to the palace, Nicholas surreptitiously took a headache pain reliever.

Tara sat beside him at the family dinner. She wore the hated glasses and another ugly dress. He wondered where she had found her wardrobe. He noticed that Michelina wore a disappointed but curious expression. His sister would demand an explanation. Later, Nicholas thought, his mind consumed with the woman beside him. She'd barely looked at him all evening. It was as if she feared everyone would know they'd been intimate if she paid him any attention.

Maggie and Michel seemed distracted. Max was squirmy, whispering to Maggie and Michel throughout the meal. The queen was having difficulty keeping the conversation going. She nodded toward one of the waiters. "You may serve dessert now please."

Maggie and Michel exchanged a secret glance. The love between them flowed like a river. Nicholas was glad his brother had found a woman who loved him for himself instead of his title. Michel's was a lonely, demanding job, but since Maggie had come into his life, Michel had never seemed happier and more complete. A stray thought about Tara flitted through Nicholas's mind, surprising him. He brushed it aside. He and Tara had a completely different arrangement, and that suited him just fine.

"Maximillian has an announcement," Michel said with pride and love in his eyes.

Everyone waited expectantly while the child lifted his chin with a happy, proud look on his face. It wasn't long ago that Max had been downcast and defeated after suffering from dyslexia. Since Maggie had come to the palace as his tutor, Max's outlook had changed from night to day.

"We're going to have a baby," he said.

The queen gasped with delight, Michelina and others made happy sounds. Nicholas glanced at Tara and caught her knowing smile. Something told him Maggie had confided in her.

"Congratulations," Nicholas said, lifting his glass of wine. "To the father, the mother and the big brother."

"How long have you known?" Queen Anna asked. "Are you taking your vitamins? Have you seen a doctor?"

Maggie laughed, and Michel put his arm around her shoulder in consolation. "She's known just a while. She hasn't seen a doctor, but she is taking her vitamins. Max and I had to persuade her to share the news with the family because she didn't want anyone fussing over her," he said, meeting his mother's gaze with a royal challenge. "I assured her that if anyone is going to fuss over her, it will be me."

Nicholas lifted his glass again in support. "Hear, hear," he said.

"Well said," Tara murmured and lifted her own glass. "Hear, hear. Congratulations."

The rest of the family toasted the pregnancy. Nicholas would have to thank his brother later for the timely distraction he had provided. With all the attention focused on Maggie and the baby, it was easy to sneak Tara away from dinner without any awkward questions.

He pulled her along beside him toward his quarters. As soon as he closed the door behind them, he took off her glasses and drew her into his arms.

"You barely said a word to me during the meal," he reproached her.

"I'm not sure how to act," she protested. "I'm supposed to be engaged, but I'm guessing we don't want everyone to know we've become intimate. I haven't figured this out yet." She looked at him in consternation. "I don't think Miss Manners has covered this one."

Nicholas laughed at the expression on her face. "Just follow my instructions."

Tara stared at him as if he were crazy. "Ha! In your dreams, Your Highness. You had me fooled for a while. I thought you didn't have any of that royal obey-me attitude, but you were just hiding it."

"Like you were hiding Maggie's secret?" Nicholas said, enjoying her flush of surprise.

"My lips are sealed," Tara said.

"Bet I can unseal them," Nicholas teased, fascinated with the prospect.

She tilted her head to one side, and the secret sensual glint flashed in her eyes. The same glint that made him want to take her against the wall. "You can try," she said, and the invitation hung between them for a microsecond before he did just that.

Tara kept him up half the night with her postvirginal curiosity. With her combination of innocence and sexuality, the woman might very well drive him mad. No sooner did he take her than he wanted her again. Nicholas had never experienced such a combination of mind-robbing fulfillment and need. They finally fell asleep in each other's arms, exhausted, but not quite sated.

The next morning, a loud knock at the door to his suite awakened them. Nicholas glanced at the clock, frowning at the early hour. He wondered if there'd been an emergency.

Rising from the bed, he grabbed a pair of shorts.

"Who is it?" Tara whispered.

"I don't know," Nicholas said, and another knock sounded.

"Your Highness, Jean Robert here by order of Her Majesty, the Queen," his mother's longtime palace assistant announced from the other side of the door.

"I'll be back in just a minute," he told Tara in a low voice. "Stay where you are." Nicholas walked from the bedroom through his den and opened the door.

"Your Highness, the queen requests your presence in her chamber immediately," Jean Robert said. "And also the presence of Miss York."

Nicholas got an uneasy feeling in his gut. "Why?"

"I am not privy to that information, sir," Jean Robert said with the discretion that had enabled him to keep his position for over thirty years. "When shall I tell her you will appear before her?"

"Give me an hour."

"As you wish, sir," Jean Robert said and bowed before he left.

Nicholas closed the door behind him and returned to Tara. She looked up at him expectantly. "What is it?"

"My mother wants you and me to appear in her chamber," Nicholas said, still mulling over what Queen Anna might want. "I told Jean Robert we would be there in an hour."

Tara's brow furrowed in confusion. "Is she always this formal?"

Nicholas nodded and shrugged. "I think it's a queen thing. Michel just picks up the phone. She doesn't usually send someone to my door at the crack of dawn, though."

"Do you think she knows we've been together?"

Nicholas rolled his eyes. "It makes no difference if she knows or doesn't. I'm a grown man. My mother may be the queen, but she sure as hell doesn't choose my lovers." He bent down to give Tara a reassuring kiss. "We can speculate forever, or we can get dressed and find out what's got her royal panties in a twist."

Tara's lips lifted in a half smile, but her eyes were full of concern.

"Don't worry. I'll take care of you," he said.

"It's not your job," she said, rising from the bed and pulling on her clothes.

Nicholas took in the proud tilt of her head and felt a rush of protectiveness. For the sake of time, he swallowed the urge to argue. It might not make sense, and Tara might disagree, but Nicholas knew it damn well was his job to take care of her.

Fifty minutes later, Tara and Nicholas were ushered into the queen's private chamber. She stood looking out a window as if she were deep in thought. As soon as she turned, Tara curtseyed. Nicholas gave a micro-bow.

Queen Anna acknowledged them and waved her hand toward the settee. "Please be seated. I must discuss with you a matter of great concern." She walked from the window to sit in a beautiful chair upholstered in a cream and burgundy tapestry.

Tara studied the queen as she appeared to collect herself. Although her classic features were still beautiful, she appeared weary and somehow older this morning. Tara thought of all the responsibility and grief the woman had carried on her slim shoulders and felt a surge of admiration and sympathy.

Queen Anna Catherine turned her gaze to Nicholas. "Miss York's father and I have spoken several times this morning. It appears that Mr. York has received some compromising photographs of you and Miss York during a late-night swim."

Tara gasped, feeling her blood drain to her feet. Nicholas covered her hand with his.

The queen paused, and her expression softened. "Would you like some tea, dear?" she asked Tara.

Tara couldn't imagine swallowing anything. She shook her head. "No, thank you, Your Majesty."

Queen Anna nodded, then turned back to Nicholas. "Mr. York is perfectly willing to pay the exorbitant sum to keep the photographs out of the media, but as we know, these pictures have a way of resurfacing. Mr. York is demanding that the two of you marry immediately, and I agree. A marriage will protect both your reputations.''

Marriage. Tara felt Nicholas's hand tighten around hers. The room began to move. Tara shook her head, and a thousand protests formed on the edge of her tongue, but she couldn't muster a sound.

''How soon can we do it?'' Nicholas asked.

Tara jerked her head to stare at him in shock. ''What!''

The queen ignored her. ''I believe the minimal necessary arrangements could be completed within three days.''

Three days! Panic roared through her. Tara's breath came in short gasps.

Nicholas glanced at her and frowned. ''She's hyperventilating. I need a paper bag.''

The room spun in circles, and her vision turned hazy. Suddenly a paper bag was pulled over her head. As if from a distance, Tara heard the voices of Nicholas and the queen.

''It will have to be a small, private affair,'' the queen said.

''I wouldn't have it any other way,'' Nicholas replied stoically.

Tara felt her cherished control of her life slipping away. She ripped the bag off her head. ''This is insane and unnecessary. The photographs can't be that bad.''

Nicholas met her gaze with eerie calm. ''Do you remember what we were wearing that night we went swimming?''

Tara's mind conjured a revealing visual. She had worn bikini panties and Nicholas had worn nothing. She felt her cheeks heat and bit her lip. "Okay, so the photographs might be embarrassing. What's the worst thing that could happen? They go into a rag sheet and are used to wrap fish and line bird cages the next day. Soon someone else is bound to offer a more enticing scandal, and this one will be history," she said breathlessly, hoping she wouldn't have to put the bag back over her head.

Nicholas turned to the queen. "Mother, she is clearly overwrought. I think it would help if I had a few moments alone with her."

The queen nodded. "Yes, but remember time is of the essence."

Nicholas shuttled Tara out the door before she could protest any further. "This is insane," she told him as he led her to his quarters. "Totally insane, and I'm not going to do it."

Nicholas shut the door behind him and pushed her into a chair. Turning his back on her as she enumerated the reasons why they shouldn't get married, he poured himself a shot glass of Scotch.

"And besides, you and I agreed that neither of us wanted to get married. You must not be too thrilled about it, either, if you're drinking Scotch before nine in the morning," she accused, wondering if she should ask him to pour her a drink too. On second thought, she'd better hold fast to her razor sharp edge of hysteria, or the queen and Nicholas would have her in front of a judge before she knew it.

He grimaced as if the liquor burned his throat. "I'm drinking because it's a special occasion."

Tara shot to her feet. "What a line! You're drinking because you know this whole thing is crazy and you don't want to marry me any more than I want to marry you. This is going to mess up all our plans."

"Not necessarily," Nicholas said. "I could be stuck with a far worse marriage partner than you, and you could be stuck with someone worse than me."

"That's a matter of opinion," she muttered.

Nicholas bared his teeth in a semblance of a smile. "Remember Dickie."

"Yes, but Dickie wasn't a prince susceptible to attacks of royal duty."

Nicholas took a calming breath and leveled his gaze at her. "You're reacting emotionally and irrationally. The best course of action for us and our respective families is for you and me to marry and do it quickly. It's my fault a photograph was taken of you with me when you were nearly naked."

Tara hated the guilt she heard in his voice. "Did you take the picture?" she asked, and shook her head. "No," she answered her own question, then asked another. "Did you force me to take off my clothes?"

"No, but I dared you and goaded you into it."

"It was my own decision."

"But I influenced you." He walked closer to her. "This is the right thing to do."

Panic sliced through her again. "How can it be right when both of us have been doing our best to avoid it?"

"There are worse possibilities," he said in that duty-bound voice she could hardly bear. "You and I understand each other, so we'll offer each other the space we need to accomplish our goals."

His words echoed in her brain like a terrible refrain. His attitude cut her to ribbons. "So I'm supposed to promise forever to you, knowing that you're thinking things could be worse?" She felt a horrible urge to cry. "This is sick. I'm calling my father," she said, and swept past him.

He caught her just as she reached the door. "Tara," he said in a low voice that got under her skin, "I do care for you."

She closed her eyes, willing the tears to wait. "You're a doctor. You care for everyone. For that matter, you care for Elvis," she said, and dashed out the door.

Tara spent the rest of the day voluntarily locked in her room while she held a series of tense, terse, emotional telephone calls with her father. She refused food, but drank four bottles of water as she paced her suite and argued with her father.

He was appalled by the photographs. She could handle his shock, but not his disappointment. He firmly agreed that the best way to neutralize the potential damage of the photographs was for her to marry Nicholas, and the sooner, the better.

Tara protested, and told her father about the medical procedure performed on her and the exciting improvement in her inner ear problem. He was cautiously hopeful, but still adamant about protecting her

reputation. She even shared the fact that she'd secretly earned two college degrees on the Internet. Although he congratulated her, he obviously didn't yet believe she could take care of herself.

His lack of confidence in her was just one more blow on a day when she didn't know if she could take any more.

"Tara," her father said, "I think you're forgetting that you are not the only consideration. There are other people involved. Have you thought about how this will affect the entire Dumont family? Have you thought about how this kind of publicity could damage Nicholas? For Pete's sake, the man is a medical doctor. He's already swimming against the tide." Her father turned silent for a moment. "How would this kind of publicity affect his credibility?"

His question immediately took the fight out of her. She felt as if her father had delivered a knockout punch. Tara sank down onto her bed.

A heavy, swollen silence hummed over the telephone line, while a collage of visuals of Nicholas raced through Tara's mind. She recalled his gentleness with the little boy in the clinic. She remembered his persistence with Cecile. She pictured his determination and passion for improving medical treatment in Marceau. He craved his freedom so that he could better serve his people. The irony of the situation hurt so much, she felt as if someone were squeezing her heart in two. She hated the very idea of being the woman who could come between him and his goal.

The tears she'd been stoically holding back began to flow down her cheeks.

"Tara," her father said. "Are you still there?"

"Yes," she said quietly, swiping her cheeks with the back of her hand.

"I'm told the wedding will be held in three days. I'll be there," he told her. "Think about what I can give you as a wedding gift. Since you're not having a large ceremony, think big," he added with forced laughter, as if to cheer her up. Her father had never understood Tara's lack of interest in exploiting his wealth.

A practical but extravagant idea came to mind. "I already know," she said, and she would love to see the surprise on her father's face. If she and Nicholas were being forced into this appalling situation, then she might as well make the most of it for both of them. "I'd like two," she said.

"Two," he echoed, confusion and surprise emanating from his voice. "Two what?"

"Two million dollars."

Ten

The white wedding dress hanging on the outside of Tara's closet door mocked her. She could almost hear it say "Na-na-na." Her instinct had been to choose something black, and Michelina had enjoyed the idea of Tara making a trendy fashion statement, but both she and Maggie had eventually vetoed it.

"First wedding," Maggie had said. "Everyone will expect you to wear white."

Everyone would expect a lot of things from her, Tara was learning. Everything had happened so quickly during the last two days, she felt as if she'd been trapped in a microwave oven. It appeared that the entire population of Marceau was more excited about this wedding than she was.

Except, perhaps, Nicholas.

She didn't know much about what he was thinking because she'd barely had more than a few minutes with him, and those few minutes hadn't offered any privacy.

Tara stared at the beautifully simple white dress and felt the sinking sensation in the pit of her stomach again that suggested she was about to make the biggest mistake of her life.

"It's beautiful," Michelina said, standing beside the bed in a rose-colored Chanel sheath. "I'm glad you went with this design, Tara. The other was too fussy." She glanced at her watch. "Only an hour to go. Your hair and makeup look fabulous. You should go ahead and get dressed."

Tara immediately shook her head. "Not yet. I, uh, don't want to mess it up."

Maggie shot her a curious look. Tara looked away, fearing Michel's wife would guess her true feelings. She'd learned Maggie was entirely too intuitive.

Maggie drew closer and took Tara's hand. Her eyes widened. "Tara, your hands are as cold as ice. Prewedding jitters?" she asked sympathetically as she briskly rubbed Tara's hand between hers.

You have no idea, Tara thought. "Maybe a few," she said, lifting her lips in a small smile.

"It's natural," Maggie soothed her. "The Dumont family can be a bit intimidating."

"In many ways, we're like a lot of other families. Dysfunctional," Michelina said. "The big differences are that we rule, we have a lot of titles, people expect a lot of us, the press is interested in the most intimate details of our lives and—"

"Michelina," Maggie cut in with a smile that didn't hide her alarm. She patted Tara's shoulder. "Tara needs reassurance right now. She needs to remember all the wonderful things about Nicholas. Tell Tara something good about Nicholas from your childhood."

Michelina furrowed her brow in concentration and paused for a moment. Her expression softened. "Okay, I have two perfect stories. When I was little, I played with dolls a lot. Sometimes they would get broken, and Nicholas would fix them. I remember he spent hours repairing my dolls. He was destined to be a people-fixer," she said with a smile. "The second story is that Nicholas secretly taught me to fence for several months until my mother found out. There's this long-standing tradition among the Dumonts that the men learn to fence, but the Dumont women aren't allowed."

"I wondered about that," Maggie said. "Michel has evaded the issue when I've asked him about it."

"It makes the men nervous," Michelina said. "I can't figure out if they're afraid the women will impale them in their sleep or if the women will hurt themselves. My mother's objection was the latter," she said with a scowl. "But Nicholas didn't see any reason why I couldn't learn. He's the least chauvinistic of my brothers, although Maggie is transforming Michel." Michelina shrugged. "Nicholas has a talent for looking beneath the surface, and he won't try to order you around too much.''

But will he ever love me? Tara's heart shook at the question. Where had it come from? she wondered, biting her lip. Love wasn't a part of this equation. This marriage was an arrangement made for the sake of protecting reputations and personal goals. Her relationship with Nicholas was a mutually beneficial agreement created out of a need for a defense against their parents' matchmaking efforts and passion.

But what about love? Her pulse raced, and she struggled with the urge to run. This was the right thing to do, Tara told herself. Nicholas might think her reputation was in danger, but Tara knew that for once, Nicholas was the one who needed protecting. And she was the woman to do it. She glanced at the wedding dress and ignored the roiling of her stomach.

She took a deep breath and stood. ''Let's get this show on the road.''

Fifty-nine minutes later, Tara's father offered his arm to her just before she was to walk down the garden pathway to where the assembled guests sat and Nicholas waited. Tamping down the voice inside her that continued to scream at her to run the other way, Tara knew she was an idiot if she didn't believe that her life was about to change.

Her father must have read the unbridelike dread on her face. He squeezed her arm and smiled encouragingly. ''Smile, Tara. I have the check for two million in my pocket, and I made it payable to you. You can think of it as mad money.''

Mad was right, she thought. This entire situation was mad, insane, crazy, wacko... She broke off her unproductive thoughts and took another deep breath. "Thank you," she said. "It's very generous of you."

"Nothing is too good for my daughter. Look, you've roped yourself a prince," he said.

When he said "rope," she pictured a noose. She smiled, however, and resolved to hold her lips in that position for the next two hours. "Let's go," she said, and they began the long walk. Nicholas's many relatives turned to look at her with happy, dreamy expressions on their faces. The queen nodded in approval.

Afraid of what she might see on Nicholas's face, Tara looked everywhere but at her bridegroom. She distracted herself from her nervousness by identifying Nicholas's brothers. The youngest, Alexander, and his adorable wife, Sophie, had rushed over from the States and arrived just last night. Tara had been told that their toddler son would be keeping an aide busy in the palace. The second born, Auguste, Marceau's military commander, sat with his wife and well-behaved daughters. Auguste's twin, Jean Marc, had flown from Washington, D.C., since he was now Marceau's diplomatic representative to the United States.

Michel stood tall and proud next to the trellis dripping in white roses. Michelina beamed her encouragement from the other side. Since Maggie was still suffering from intermittent morning sickness, Michelina had been chosen as Tara's maid of honor. Next to her stood the minister who was to perform the nuptial rites, his balding head gleaming in the sunlight.

Tara felt the intensity of Nicholas's gaze so strongly he might as well have called her name. Unable to ignore the call, she finally looked at him. Dressed in a tuxedo, he emanated strength and intelligence. And commitment.

Tara's breath stopped at the expression in his eyes. She could almost believe he genuinely cared for her. She could almost believe he wanted this. If she didn't know better, she would think that Nicholas almost loved— Her heart palpitated and she took a quick breath. It wasn't possible, she told herself. He was just a very good actor. He might have hated all those years of making personal appearances in the name of royal duty, but today the practice was paying off in spades.

The closer she walked to Nicholas, the more the whole scene seemed to take on an otherworldly sensation. This was someone else's world, someone else's wedding. After the minister greeted the guests, asked who gives this bride, and her father joined her hand with Nicholas's, however, Tara was slammed back into reality. This was her world and her wedding.

The minister could have spoken in Greek for all she took in during the next few moments. She somehow managed to repeat her vows, and she noticed the concern on Nicholas's face. It was as if he knew she'd hike up her dress and run away if given half a chance. When he placed the diamond-encrusted band, clearly a family heirloom, on her finger, she was filled with guilt. This ring didn't belong to her. It belonged to the woman whom Nicholas would someday love.

The minister pronounced them man and wife, and Nicholas drew her into his arms and kissed her. She felt the promise in his caress, and the duty. The assault of a dozen different emotions nearly undid her. Her eyes filled with tears. Nicholas brushed his fingertip under her eye and bent his head close to hers.

"It will be okay," he whispered, but even though the diamonds in her ring were the best and most authentic, Tara felt like a fraud.

The reception passed in a blur. She wasn't sure how she did it, but she danced and smiled as expected. Hours later, Michelina hustled her into her going-away dress, and Nicholas guided her up the ramp to the royal yacht that would take them to the open seas for the next two days.

He slid his arm around her waist. "Wave and smile for the cameras. It's almost over."

"And then what?" Tara murmured to herself, but did as Nicholas suggested. The yacht left the dock long after her arm grew tired, and she felt her smile begin to droop. Then, with the exception of ten crew members, she and Nicholas were finally alone. Under other circumstances, the ocean breeze would have been refreshing, but Tara just felt numb.

"What do you want to do?" Nicholas asked. "Are you hungry? Do you want to change clothes?" The silence stretched between them, and he gave a wry chuckle. "Wanna go for a nude swim?"

Tara shot him a dark look. "I believe that's what got us into this predicament." She closed her eyes and sighed. "I think going to bed is a good idea."

Another long silence followed, and Tara felt her stomach tense. She opened her eyes to meet his gaze and saw a combination of curiosity and sexual intent. Her breath hitched in her throat, and she felt an attack of nerves. "Go to bed to rest," she clarified quickly. "To sleep. To take a nap."

He nodded slowly. "Okay, let me show you to the suite."

As he led her around the deck, Tara struggled with her trepidation about making love with Nicholas. After all, it wouldn't be the first time. But it somehow seemed very different now that they were married, she thought as she followed Nicholas into the spacious, lush suite.

The large bed drew her gaze like a magnet. She would share that bed with Nicholas as his wife. Anticipation, expectation, hung heavily in the air like humidity before a storm.

Pushing aside the feelings that tugged at her, she looked around the rest of the tastefully decorated suite. She caught sight of flowers, champagne in an ice bucket and, most important, her luggage. "Oh good," she said, striding across the room. "The luggage is here, so I'll just grab some comfortable clothes and change in the—"

Nicholas was by her side, picking up the suitcase just as she touched it. "A bride shouldn't be lifting luggage."

Tara blinked in surprise. "Thank you," she murmured as he placed the suitcase on a luggage stand.

"You're welcome." He studied her with an unreadable expression on his face, then he leaned forward and dipped his mouth over hers for a kiss that almost lingered. "Get some rest," he said, as if she would need plenty of stamina later, then walked out of the room.

Tara's heart hammered in her chest. Had his gaze oozed sexual intent? Or was that her imagination? And how did she feel about it? She groaned. Too many questions! The last few days had been such a whirlwind, she hadn't had time to answer those kinds of questions, and she didn't have the energy right now. Now, she was going to rest, she told herself firmly.

After unzipping her suitcase, she was greeted with another surprise. No cotton pajamas. She saw Michelina's fine hand in the choice of lingerie. Silk, satin, revealing, seductive. Perfect for someone else's honeymoon.

Hours later, Nicholas arranged for dinner to be brought to their suite. He was watching her as Tara awakened because the dinner cart wheel squeaked loudly.

She lifted her head from the satin pillow and pushed her hair from her face. Her eyes were sleepy, her hair tousled and whatever she was wearing looked slippery and sexy. Nicholas felt a surge of possessiveness. She was his wife. The marriage sure as hell hadn't been his first choice for the outcome of their relationship, but it hadn't dampened his desire for her either.

Her gaze connected with his, then skittered away. "I'm afraid to ask how long I've been asleep," she said, rising to a sitting position.

"Are you sure you're no relation to Rip van Winkle?" he teased, pulling the champagne bottle from the bucket. "Would you like some dinner?"

Tara covered a yawn and nodded.

The sheet dropped to her lap, and Nicholas got another teasing image of her blue silk chemise. The material must have shifted in her sleep. The shadow of one dusky nipple taunted him. Nicholas remembered how her breast felt in his hand. He remembered her sexy restlessness when he drew her nipple into his mouth. He remembered how wet and tight she felt around him. He felt himself turn hard.

Tara must have read his expression. She glanced down and quickly adjusted her gown. Biting her lip, she turned her attention to the dinner cart. "Oh, lobster," she said, licking her lips in anticipation.

Something uncivilized and primitive rippled through him. Nicholas struggled with the urge to tear off that scanty bit of silk and the veil of discomfort between them.

"I don't think I ate more than a bite of cake at the reception, and that was for the photographer." She slid out of bed and quickly grabbed a robe.

Nicholas would have preferred her completely naked beneath him, but he bided his time. "Champagne?" he asked, and pulled it from the bucket.

"No disagreement from me," she said, lifting their glasses to catch the liquid when he popped the bottle open.

Replacing the bottle in the bucket, he lifted his glass to hers in a toast. "To us—for surviving the last seventy-two hours."

Tara nodded as if she didn't totally agree, but took a sip anyway. He pulled out her chair, and she sat down at the table and took another swallow of champagne. She licked her lips afterward, and her robe gaped to reveal the swell of one breast.

Nicholas took a deep breath and a long swallow of the bubbly liquid for fortification. He watched Tara lift a bite of lobster to her lips, and as she sucked it gently inside, Nicholas prepared himself for an hour of torture.

Everything she ate made his blood pressure rise another notch. She licked hollandaise sauce from the asparagus before she took it into her mouth. She took intermittent bites of lobster dipped in butter, and he would swear she moaned every time. The sounds of her gastronomic pleasure made him so hard he could barely sit.

After she finished the lobster, she looked at the chocolate hazelnut torte and shook her head. "I know I can't eat all of that."

"We can share," he said, plunging his fork into a slice of the torte and lifting a bite to her lips.

She looked at him in surprise, but opened her

mouth. As the morsel melted in her mouth, she moaned.

The woman was going to kill him, he thought.

"That was so good."

"Better than the wedding cake," he acknowledged, taking a bite even though he was much more interested in sating a completely different appetite.

She turned silent, and her eyes darkened with sadness. He immediately sensed her tension and unhappiness.

"I'm sorry," she said, misery filling her voice.

"Sorry for what?"

"I'm sorry we had to get married."

She was too far away, he thought. She'd been too far away ever since they'd decided to marry. Nicholas rounded the table and picked her up in his arms.

She stiffened. "What are you doing?"

"I think that's obvious," he said, lowering her to the bed. "I'm putting you to bed." He grabbed their champagne glasses and joined her. "Stop feeling responsible. The photos were taken of both of us. As I told you before, there are far worse things than you and I getting married."

She frowned, but accepted the glass and took a sip. "Far worse things. That doesn't really help."

"Okay. Then how about saying that this arrangement has its compensations?"

Taking another sip, she met his gaze. Her eyes were both wary and sexy. She parted her lips.

"Don't lick them," he said.

Her eyes widened in surprise. "Why not?"

"Because I want to.

Eleven

Nicholas lowered his head and ran his tongue over her champagne-wet lips. Tara paused for a long moment as if she were undecided, then she tilted her mouth for better access.

The gesture of welcome shot heat through his groin like an intimate touch from her hand. Nicholas consumed her lips the same way he planned to consume her body. She opened her mouth, and he dipped his tongue inside to explore, to take, to mate.

He felt her fingers climb up the nape of his neck and deepened the kiss. She moaned, the same sensual sound of pleasure she'd made earlier. The sound vibrated throughout him, cranking his arousal up another notch.

She pulled back slightly and took a quick breath.

"How will I know when you're doing something because of duty and when you're not?" she asked breathlessly.

Nicholas gave a rough chuckle and set his glass of champagne on the nightstand. He undid the belt of her robe and took her glass. "There are some things a man can't hide, *chérie*."

"But I—"

He rubbed her lips with his index finger. "Unbutton my shirt," he said in a low voice.

She paused a long moment, then did as he asked, skimming her hand down his chest. She went a step farther and pushed the shirt from his shoulders. Meeting his gaze, she slowly lowered her hands to the top of his slacks.

He rubbed his finger over her mouth again.

She darted her tongue over the tip, sending his temperature up ten degrees. Seeing the dare in her eyes, he pushed his finger in her mouth. Tara licked it the same way she would...

Nicholas's restraint ran thin. He took a gulp from her glass and felt her unfasten his slacks. Something inside him tore open. He pulled his finger from her decadent mouth, and in one motion, he pushed her robe and chemise down to her hips. There was just a little champagne left in the bottom of the flute. Following his instincts, he took her mouth and spilled the rest of the liquid over her breasts.

He caught her gasp with a French kiss, then lowered his lips to taste the heady combination of champagne and Tara's skin. He took the nipple that had taunted him earlier deep into his mouth, groaning at the sensation. "I've been wanting to do that all night," he muttered, and looked into her eyes, which were darkening with desire.

She bit her lip and shifted restlessly, a little sign of arousal that excited him even more. Something about this woman made him want to learn all her secrets. He wanted to be the man to put her over the edge. He wanted to be the man in whom she confided. "What else have you been wanting to do all night?" she asked, and that was all the invitation he needed.

He rid himself of the rest of his clothes and devoted himself to learning every inch of her body. He found out that kissing her nipple then blowing on it made her wriggle with pleasure. He found out that open-mouthed kisses on her abdomen almost tickled her. He also learned that her femininity bloomed like a flower when he sank his fingers into her wetness and stroked and caressed her.

He learned that when Tara grew impatient, her kisses were so wild and hot he wondered if he could get scorched. Her hands were eager and bold on his arousal. Just when he thought he couldn't bear one more stroke from her taunting fingertips, she lifted a finger, damp with the honey of his desire, to her lips.

So aroused he thought he would explode, Nicholas rolled them both over so that she straddled his hips. "Are you ready?"

Her lips swollen and her eyes hazy with passion,

she nodded. Grasping her hips with his hands, he lowered her onto his aching, straining shaft. She closed her eyes and expelled a sexy sigh at their joining.

She was wet and tight, gripping him like a velvet glove. She felt so good, he was pushed to the edge of reason. She began to undulate over him, and he guided her hips for maximum pleasure. He watched her breasts dip and sway with her movements, but it was the expression on her face that compelled him. She was totally focused on him, she was a part of him. Everything she felt was written in her eyes: trust, hope, passion and something deep and ageless.

He felt a rush of primitive possession and something tender he couldn't quite identify. So much of their marriage had been a pretense for the sake of others. But this was real.

Her breath shortened and her eyes dropped to half-mast. She accelerated her movements, and he felt the beginning of her completion with her tiny, intimate clenches. The sight and feel of her sent him flying, and his climax was so powerful it rolled through him like thunder.

Tara collapsed on his chest, and Nicholas tried to catch his breath and a sliver of sanity. In the most basic, elemental way, he had taken her as his wife. With the taking, though, he could have almost sworn he heard a door locking behind him. A whisper slipped through the keyhole. Everything would be different for both of them now. He fought the possibility, making a silent oath to himself and that disturbing whisper. He had made a previous commitment before Tara had come into his life, and that would never change.

The following morning, Tara awakened just as the sun began to peek through the curtains on the windows. Her body was turned toward Nicholas almost the same way a flower turned toward the sun. She indulged the secret opportunity to look at him while he slept. His hair was attractively sleep-tousled, his profile aristocratic. His lips were full and sensual, his chin stubborn. He was such a strong yet gentle man. He was the most mentally fierce man she'd ever met. It was amazing to her that he could be so voracious for her. Last night, it was as if he couldn't get enough of her. He had been determined to learn every part of her body, and he had made her so hot she hadn't known where she ended and he began. And she had been consumed with meeting his every need.

It was as if everything she felt she couldn't say aloud to him she could say with her body.

Tara's heart squeezed painfully in her chest. She was very afraid. What she felt for Nicholas was so powerful that it shook her. She was afraid she had done what she'd sworn she wouldn't do. She was afraid she had fallen in love with him.

She saw Nicholas's eyes blink open and shut several times. He turned his head and gazed at her with his penetrating light blue eyes. "How long have you been watching me?" he asked, and pulled her toward him.

The expression in his eyes made her heart turn over. "Just a couple of minutes. I was wondering if you might like some breakfast."

He slid his hand down her hip. "Afterward," he told her, and drove all thoughts of food from her head.

If Tara could choose a day to seal in a scrapbook forever, it would be this day. Later, she and Nicholas shared breakfast in bed, then took a swim in the ocean. Nicholas tried to talk her into a nude swim, but had to content himself with stealing her bathing suit top until it was time to climb back on the yacht. They laughed and joked with each other, temporarily shelving more weighty concerns.

They shared dinner on the deck and she sat in his arms as they watched the sun set. Tara had the nagging premonition that once they returned to Marceau and the palace tomorrow, everything would be different.

"You're quiet," Nicholas murmured, fanning his fingers through her hair.

"It's been such a fabulous day. I hate for it to end," she said, tucking her head into his throat and inhaling his clean, male scent.

"Can't play forever," he said.

"No. I hope the adjustments won't be too difficult."

"They shouldn't be," he said with a shrug. "I'm not the most visible royal. If the palace PR department tries to book up too much of your time for appearances, tell them to stuff it."

"I really do want to finish my thesis. I've had a

few distractions recently that have kept me from making any progress."

"Distractions? You're kidding," he teased, squeezing her waist. "A little thing like marrying me."

She looked up at him and smiled. "Oh, I would say you're plenty distracting."

He brushed a kiss over her forehead. "I'll be out of your way day after tomorrow. I'm headed back to a free clinic on the other side of the island."

"I'd love to go with you," she said wistfully.

"Didn't you just say you wanted to complete your thesis?" he asked, brushing her nose with his forefinger.

"Yes," she said reluctantly. "But visiting a clinic with you is a fun distraction." She looked into his face and dreaded him leaving. How silly, she thought. She should be relieved. "Do you worry about this turning out all right?"

"You mean our marriage," he said. "I told you. It could end up being the best of two worlds. You'll stay out of my way so I can achieve my goals, and I'll do the same for you. We'll allow each other the independence we crave. We understand each other. We have passion without the complications of emotion. There are some distinct advantages to the fact that you and I didn't marry for love."

Tara felt a cold chill run through her. Nicholas had assured her that she wouldn't fall in love with him, but she wasn't sure how to stop herself. She sensed it would really upset him if he knew her emotions were involved in a major way. Her heart twisted with the same fear she'd pushed aside this morning. She needed to find a way not to love him.

Within eighteen hours, Nicholas and Tara were waving at the paparazzi as the yacht pulled into shore. Whisked off to the palace, they attended another party planned to celebrate their marriage and homecoming.

Nicholas dutifully stood by Tara's side and accepted congratulations and teasing remarks about the end of his bachelor days. At last, the party ended, and he and Tara retreated to his quarters.

He looked at Tara as she sat in the middle of his bed wearing a silky gown and emotion in her eyes that both warmed him and disturbed him. He couldn't help feeling torn.

She scooted to the edge and crooked her finger for him to come closer. "What?" he asked, allowing himself to be lured for the moment.

She smiled and lifted her fingers to loosen his tie. "I'm going to help you get rid of your tie and shirt. Isn't that what good wives do?"

"It's not a bad start," he said, feeling arousal hum through him as she unbuttoned his shirt.

"The last few days have been so wonderful, I don't want them to end." She slid her finger down his chest to the top of his belt and looked up at him through the dark fringe of her eyelashes. "If you won't let me go with you tomorrow, will you tell me which clinic you'll be visiting?"

His heart gave an odd twist. "You are really interested in what I do, aren't you?"

She wrinkled her brow in confusion. "Of course I am. You make a difference in people's lives. You meet interesting people with problems and help solve them. How could I not be interested?"

Nicholas felt the twisting sensation again and lifted his hand to touch her silky hair. "Every other woman my mother has thrown at me has been bored to tears by my interest in medicine. Why are you different?"

She shrugged and chuckled. "Oops. I tried to warn you, but it's a little late now. You're married to a weirdo."

Weirdo. He damn well liked her kind of weird. He had never thought he would find a woman with whom he could share his passion for his work. Never. Tara was such a compelling mix of qualities. Her genuine interest and honesty were like pure oxygen to him. Nicholas couldn't help admiring her determination to get her education. It was more than admiration. He understood her need to become something different from what was expected of her. That same need echoed inside him.

He wanted to take her with him to the clinic tomorrow, but something stopped him. If he believed love and a conventional marriage wouldn't keep him from his goals, she would be an ideal wife except for the fact that she was damn distracting to him. Even now, he felt the same regret she'd just expressed about their honeymoon ending. She underestimated her appeal, he thought. She underestimated her power. She knew what was important. Her lack of absorption with her appearance only made her more seductive to him. He wanted her laughter, her tears, her trust. He could spend entirely too much time wanting her even though he could have her in his bed every night.

Alarm tightened into a knot in his chest. He couldn't be sidetracked. He could give Tara his affection, but his head and his heart were his own.

The following morning, Nicholas left their bed by 6:00 a.m. to travel to the other side of the island to work in a free clinic. Tara scolded herself for missing him and took her breakfast in her room. She turned on her computer to delve back into her thesis. Just as she began to make progress, a knock sounded at the door. Tara opened the door to a young woman.

"Your Highness, I am Ana Reeves and I have been assigned the great honor of being your palace aide."

This was news to Tara. She extended her hand. "I'm pleased to meet you, Ana. I must confess I don't expect to have the same schedule of duties the other royal family members have, so I don't plan to give you much work."

Ana shook her head. "Oh, no, ma'am. If you'll pardon me for saying so, you're already scheduled through next month."

Tara blinked. "Excuse me? No one told me I was scheduled for anything."

Ana smiled. "That's my job, ma'am. You're in great demand because you're the newest wife of a Dumont. Prince Nicholas has always been a bit elusive, so I imagine people feel that by meeting you, they are, in a way, meeting him. I see you're already dressed. Princess Maggie is feeling a bit under the weather from morning sickness, and she asked if you might consider taking her place at tea with a local women's club.''

Tara swallowed her dismay. She'd rather get a tooth pulled. ''I—I—I'm not sure I have anything to wear,'' she protested.

''I'm told Princess Michelina purchased some wardrobe additions in your absence. Have you checked your closet?''

''No,'' Tara said, confused. ''Just a second.'' She hurried to the large walk-in closet in Nicholas's bedroom. She'd been so busy since she set foot in the palace yesterday that she hadn't unpacked, and this morning, she'd pulled on shorts and a top from a dresser drawer. Tara flung open the closet door, flicked on the light and gazed at her side of the closet. She blinked, unable to find any of the garments she'd brought with her. Instead, more than two dozen new designer outfits hung in their place. Although she knew Michelina meant well, she felt a twinge of resentment.

Slowly she returned to her new aide. ''It appears Michelina has been shopping.''

''Yes. Her taste is exquisite. Shall I tell Princess Maggie's aide that you will attend the tea?''

Tara hesitated. She hadn't taken the time to decide how many royal duties she wanted to take on. On the other hand, she liked Maggie very much and wouldn't dream of letting her down. She sighed. ''I'll do it. Just this once,'' she said.

Ana beamed and clasped her hands together. "She'll be so grateful. Now let me get your appointment book."

After that, Tara felt as if she'd stepped on a motorized banana peel that never stopped. Inundated with invitations, Tara found her schedule packed to the brim. When asked questions about Nicholas, she quickly learned the art of saying something without revealing anything. The questions, however, reminded her that her marriage was in many ways a sham. There was so much she didn't know about the man she called husband.

She tried not to think about the fact that Nicholas was gone nearly every day, even on the weekends. The only time she saw him was during dinner with the family or at night when he physically reminded her of their vows by making love to her.

Craving more of him, she asked him about his day, and he told her stories about the children he treated, and the other doctors who contributed to the free clinics. Tara found herself envying his time away from palace protocol, and was appalled with herself. She knew those feelings were dangerous, because Nicholas had been straight about his priorities from the beginning and she'd accepted them. She desperately needed a change of pace.

One night after they'd made love, she curled against him. "Nicholas, let me go with you tomorrow."

He turned still and silent. "I won't be home until very late."

"That's okay. I just want to go with you for a change. I'll stay out of the way or help patients with their medical forms, but I really want to go."

"But, Tara, I thought you've been wanting to work on your thesis. I haven't heard you talk about it at all, lately."

His objections made her stomach knot, but she was determined. "I haven't had time because of all my royal obligations."

"Tell them to clear your schedule," he said, then ran his hand through her hair. "You're allowing me to accomplish the things that are important to me. I promised you I would do the same for you."

Tara sighed. She couldn't argue his point without revealing the fact that she simply wanted to spend time with him, and if she revealed that, he might guess that she loved him, and things between them would be even worse. Frustrated, she stayed awake, trying not to feel the way she felt.

Tell them to clear your schedule. Easier said than done. Everyone always wanted an explanation, and she couldn't provide one without revealing her goal of earning her master's degree. Even then, she doubted that her education would be considered a valid excuse if duty called.

Every night, Tara asked Nicholas if she could join him the following day, but he always had an excuse. After the fifth night, she was so hurt, she hid in the bathroom and cried. When Nicholas kissed her before he left the next morning, she pretended to be asleep. As soon as he left, she stared at the designer dress hanging outside the closet door. She was scheduled to wear that dress to several activities today where she would pretend to be Nicholas's happy wife.

The truth was, she didn't feel at all like Nicholas's wife, and she certainly didn't feel happy. She felt as if she were wearing someone else's clothes and living someone else's life. Tara felt as if she were drowning.

Was this how the rest of her life would be? Pretending not to love Nicholas, pretending to be someone else? The possibility terrified her so that she felt she could hardly breathe.

Willing herself to calm down, she knew she had to do something drastic. Soon.

Twelve

One week later, Nicholas checked the results on a strep test and wrote the prescription for his droopy ten-year-old female patient as he pulled a blanket around her. "She needs to start taking this immediately and finish all of it even after she starts to feel better," he said to the girl's mother.

"Thank you, Doctor," the woman murmured.

Just as she and her daughter left, Fred entered the makeshift examination room. Nicholas's bodyguard wore an expression of concern as he gave a quick nod. "Your Highness," he said.

"Problem?" Nicholas asked.

"It's your wife, sir," Fred said.

Nicholas's chest twisted like a vice. "Tara? What's wrong? Has there been an accident?"

"No accident has been reported, but she's missing."

"Missing?" Nicholas echoed, alarm slamming into him. "What do you mean, missing?"

"We don't know, but we thought you should be informed. Your wife canceled her scheduled appointments, made a trip to the bank, then stopped by a clothing shop. Her escort lost track of her after that."

Nicholas racked his brain for what could have happened to Tara. Every possibility raced through his mind. What if she'd been kidnapped? His blood ran cold. He rubbed his face. That would be the worst, he thought. He couldn't avoid a twist of discomfort over some of the things she'd told him recently. She'd felt overwhelmed by all the requests for her appearance at various functions, and she hadn't been pleased with her progress on her thesis. She'd repeatedly asked to join him and he'd refused. Nicholas's stomach turned. An unwelcome possibility slithered through his mind like a serpent. What if she'd left him?

He turned to Fred. "We're returning to the palace now."

During the drive home, Nicholas brooded over Tara. He'd been so determined to prove to himself that marriage wouldn't get in the way of his goal of jump-starting the free medical clinics that he'd ignored every warning flag she'd waved. How many times had he ducked her request to join him during one of his clinic days? A bitter taste filled his mouth. She didn't know how distracting he found her. She didn't know that he wasn't sure he would be able to keep his mind on the job if she was near. She didn't know because he sure hadn't told her. The knowledge scared the hell out of him.

He remembered the brief, odd conversation they'd shared this morning before he'd left. Her eyes still sleepy, she'd lifted her arms to embrace him. He remembered how tempted he'd been to crawl back into bed with her.

"Tell me what you like about me," she'd whispered.

An edgy discomfort had twisted through him. If he told her how many things he liked about her, they'd be there all day. Instead, he'd chuckled as he hugged her. "I like the honesty I see in your eyes," he'd said, inhaling her scent. "And I like the way your hair smells. Work on your thesis some today."

He'd left her, feeling as if she'd wanted more from him, needed more. If there'd been nothing inside him to give, he might have dismissed the feeling, but Nicholas felt far more for Tara than he'd been willing to admit, even to himself.

As soon as he arrived at the palace, he brushed past the queen's aide and Michel's inquiring gaze. He strode to the suite he'd shared with Tara for the last month and immediately spotted an envelope with his name on it propped on the bed where they'd made love.

Nicholas tore open the envelope and held his breath as he read Tara's message.

Dear Nicholas,

I've decided to take a sabbatical from palace duty. With each passing day, it seems I slide further and further from my goal of finishing my thesis, and I can't help feeling less of myself. I didn't want to burden you with this, so I made arrangements with the university sponsoring my online classes to spend the summer on campus. I'm hoping I can follow your example of achievement.

In the meantime, I've set up a charitable foundation for the free clinics. You should receive the information by courier this afternoon. Maybe you can think of it as my dowry. Please know you have my admiration and love. We can figure out what to do about our ''arrangement'' later.

Love,
Tara

Nicholas's chest physically hurt. A wrenching sensation tore through his gut. What if he'd lost her before he'd really even known he had her?

''Nicholas.''

Nicholas heard Michel's voice from just a few steps away. ''Is Tara okay?''

Nicholas paced the bedroom, looking for signs of her. It appeared she'd left most of her belongings. ''Probably,'' he said, checking the closet. All her clothes hung there as if she would return any minute. ''She didn't want anyone to know, but she's working on her master's degree. She hasn't been able to get anything done because of all the ceremonial appearances she's had to make." He went into the bathroom and saw some of her toiletries on the counter. Checking the shower, he saw her shampoo.

I love the way your hair smells. His words from this morning haunted him.

"Where is she?" Michel asked, standing just outside the bathroom door. "And for heaven's sake, what are you looking for?"

"I don't know what I'm looking for," Nicholas said. But deep inside he knew he was looking for a sign that she wasn't truly gone. "She left to attend summer session at a university."

"Which one?" Michel asked, exasperation creeping into his voice.

"I don't know." He felt like a caged animal.

Silence followed. "Your wife has left the country to attend a university and you don't know where it is?"

"I've been busy," he said, and knew the response was lame before it left his lips.

Michel lifted a dark brow. "Perhaps too busy."

Nicholas stiffened. "Perhaps," he conceded.

"What are you going to do?"

Nicholas swore. "I don't know. She kept asking to visit a clinic with me, and I wouldn't let her because I get distracted as hell around her. Plus, I've been damn determined to get the free clinic program off the ground."

"Did you tell her?"

"Tell her what?"

Michel's jaw clenched with stretched patience. Nicholas saw the warning signs, but at the moment he didn't care.

"Did you tell her *why* you didn't want her to visit a clinic with you?"

"No," he admitted, calling himself a fool. He sank down on the bed.

Michel sighed and walked to stand in front of him. "It's none of my business except for the fact that you're my brother, and I wouldn't call myself an expert on women, but Maggie tells me American women want show-and-tell. They want the words, the actions. They want it all. The flip side is they give everything in return."

He hadn't thought he wanted everything from Tara. In fact, he'd told himself and her he hadn't wanted much from her at all. "Ass," he called himself under his breath and raked his hand through his hair. "I didn't want to get emotionally involved with her."

"With *your wife?*" Michel asked in an incredulous tone.

"I didn't want to get sidetracked from getting the free clinic program off the ground."

"Oh," Michel said. "You thought you would have to choose between your passion for your woman and your passion for your career."

Surprised at his brother's understanding, he looked up. "Yes, how did you—" He broke off, recalling that his brother's position as future ruler of Marceau was just as consuming as Nicholas's. His brother was totally in love with his wife, and had in fact lightened up quite a bit since Maggie had come into his life. "So how did you do it?"

"I have never wanted a woman the way I wanted Maggie. Having her with me is the difference between living and just existing. She fulfills me as a man. I'm better because of her, and I will do anything to keep her."

That night when Nicholas went to bed alone and Tara wasn't there to question him about his day, Michel's words played through Nicholas's mind. Why had he fought this? he wondered, and knew it was fear. He hated seeing it in himself. He inhaled deeply, searching for a whiff of her scent on the pillow. An image of her smile floated through his tortured mind, her laughter echoed inside him. Her tenderness.

His chest twisted tight with a sense of loss. What had he done? She had been his for the taking, and that was all he'd done. Take. How in the world could he get her back?

Three days after she'd fled Marceau, Tara carried her two bags of groceries up the stairs to her second-floor apartment. A lot had happened during the last three days. After she'd made flight arrangements and set up the charitable foundation at the bank for the free clinics, she'd ditched her escort by exiting through the back door of a busy boutique and quickly gotten a taxi. Within an hour and a half, she'd taken a seat over the wing of a Boeing 747 jet armed with her laptop, which she'd stashed in a large purse, along with credit cards, passport and toothbrush.

Although Tara had tried not to look back, she had trouble falling asleep at night. She told herself it was the time zone change. It wasn't Nicholas. After all, she'd barely spent any time with him even if she had fallen in love with him.

She fumbled for her keys in her purse as she stopped in front of her door. Balancing both bags on her hips, she stuck the key in the door and was puzzled when the knob turned so easily. It was almost as if she'd forgotten to lock it, which was entirely possible, she supposed, not alarmed. The great thing about Groton Hills, Idaho, was the insulated nature of the small, college town.

She nudged the door open with her knee, then made a quick dash for the kitchen counter, colliding with an all-too-familiar male body. The impact took her breath and sent her groceries tumbling to the floor.

"Milk, eggs," she said desperately, unable to tear her gaze from the man who had filled her heart and mind even with half a world between them. Her heart pounded in her chest. "Nicholas, what are you doing here?"

At the same time, he said, "Why did you set up the foundation?"

He looked travel-weary, and she couldn't stop looking at him. Tara tried to muster some restraint, but she'd never imagined she could miss someone so much.

"I'm here to see you," he said, revealing nothing.

"But how did you get into my apartment?"

"Fred broke in for me. He's handy, that way." He nodded toward the back of the building. "I asked him to wait outside."

She nodded, still wondering why Nicholas was standing in front of her.

"Everyone was worried when you left," he said.

Tara took a careful breath and glanced downward, spotting the leaking milk container. Grateful for the distraction, she quickly scooped it up and put it in the sink. "I'm sorry. I didn't want anyone to worry, but I had to do it quickly, or I knew I wouldn't do it all. It was so easy to get drawn into the never-ending schedule of appointments, and—"

Nicholas slid his arm around her from behind. "Why did you leave me?"

Her heart stalled and she bit her lip. "I didn't leave you, per se. I left so I could finish my thesis."

He slowly turned her around. "Are you sure you didn't leave because I wasn't around more?"

She shook her head because she couldn't tell him the truth. Not this time. "No, I just—"

"Because I've been a fool," he said quietly with eyes so honest and intense she felt as if he were burning past her pretense with a blue flame.

"Fool?" she finally managed.

"When I was lying in bed the other night, I tried to pinpoint the moment you got into my heart. I wondered if it was after we came back from the honeymoon, when we lay in the dark and you would ask me questions. I was usually dead on my feet, but the sound of your voice and the feel of you in my arms gave me peace. Knowing you would be there made all the difference in the world,'' he said.

Tara's heart swelled in her chest, and a tiny seed of hope grew inside her. "Why didn't you tell me this?"

He scowled. "Because I was fighting it. I'd convinced myself that I couldn't devote myself to a woman and to launching the free clinic project at the same time. I couldn't divide myself that way. That was part of the reason I didn't want you to visit the clinics with me."

Remembered hurt stabbed her. "I don't understand," she said. "You let me go with you once, and I didn't get in the way."

Nicholas swore under his breath. "You were never in the way, but my feelings for you grew. I couldn't be in the same room with you without wanting to focus my entire attention on you. All I wanted was to get you alone. I couldn't imagine attending to patients if you were anywhere near."

Tara shook her head in disbelief. "I can't believe I had that much of an effect on you. You were gone every day until late at night, even on the weekends."

"Running," he said, lifting his hand to her cheek, "from something so powerful it scared the hell out of me. I tried to tell myself that I just wanted you, but you didn't just get under my skin, Tara. You got into my heart. I can't let you go."

A knot formed in her throat, and Tara's eyes burned with the threat of tears. She struggled with elation and fear. "I don't think I can go back to Marceau," she said. "I'll get in your way, and I can't bear the idea of keeping you from a goal you've had for so many years.

"Which brings up the question I asked you just a few moments ago. Why did you set up the charitable foundation?"

She shrugged. "It seemed like the right thing to do. My father asked me what I wanted as a wedding gift, and I told him two million dollars. I figured it would be a good start for you."

Nicholas shook his head. "A two-million-dollar wedding gift. In your letter you called it a dowry. What if I want the woman a lot more than the dowry? I want more than nights with you. I want a life with you."

Tears spilled over, and she began to tremble. She was still afraid to hope. "But what about your project?"

"I don't have to work seven days a week on it. I can't," he said, pulling her into his arms. "As important to me as this is, I can't do it by myself, and I've found some colleagues who are as committed to the project as I am. Two of them even agreed to handle the coordination while I'm away most of the summer."

Tara blinked in surprise and pulled back slightly to look at him. "Most of the summer?"

He met her gaze with dead-on commitment. "I plan to spend the summer with my wife while she finishes her master's degree."

Her heart stuttered. "Nicholas, you can't just sit here while I'm working on my thesis."

"You're right. There's a teaching medical center thirty miles from here. I plan to assist a colleague who specializes in gerontology three days a week. That will give you time to work on your thesis without me interrupting you," he said with a slight grin, then turned serious. "It will also give you and me time to stop pretending we don't love each other."

Tara bit her lip and blinked back another spate of tears.

"*Chérie,* you're killing me with your tears. Are you happy or sad?"

"Happy, I think," she said. "I couldn't even allow myself to hope that you would love me."

"You know you left your shampoo," he told her.

Tara blinked at the abrupt change in subject. "I left most of my things."

"I missed you so much when you left that I got up in the middle of the night to smell your shampoo. But it's just not the same as when its scent is on your hair. Tara, forgive me. Give me a chance to win you."

"Oh, Nicholas," she said, her heart so full she thought it might burst, "you won me a long time ago."

"Then give me a chance to spend my life winning you, and let me start now."

"Oh, yes," she said, feeling as if the stars were clicking into alignment as he dipped his head to kiss her.

He scooped her up into his arms and walked toward the back of the apartment. "It can't possibly get better than this," she murmured more to herself than him. "Not possibly."

"Yes, it can. When we return to Marceau, we're moving out of the palace. The palace was fine for my bachelor days, but I want more privacy for you and me now. Especially in the current emotional climate."

"What's wrong?" she asked, lifting her fingertip to the frown between his eyebrows. "Problems between Michelina and the queen?"

"World War Three," he said, setting her down on the bed. "My mother has been waiting none too patiently for more news from the private investigator about my brother Jacques."

"This is the one you all thought had drowned?"

He nodded, jerking loose his tie and unbuttoning his shirt. "My mother hasn't wanted to tell Michelina because my sister has been so flighty and temperamental lately, so she held a private meeting with the Dumont men and told us that the investigator believes Jacques may be living in the United States."

Although she was distracted by the sight of his muscular chest, Tara felt a sliver of surprise. "Wouldn't that be amazing if you could find him? Can you imagine what he's doing?"

"We don't know much except that his adoptive father was a fisherman in the Caribbean and they migrated to the United States."

"So why is Michelina upset?"

Nicholas made a face. "She found out about the

private meeting and popped a cork. My mother is afraid she's about to run away. When they're in the same room, they're either arguing with each other or not speaking at all,'' he said, diverting her attention as he started to unfasten his slacks. ''One more reason we don't need to be at the palace 24/7.'' He pushed his slacks and briefs down his legs, and Tara was reminded again of what an impressive virile body he had.

''You're overdressed,'' he told her, joining her on the bed. He lifted her shirt over her head, then went to work on her jeans. ''I need to be as close to you as I can get.''

Tara felt a drumbeat start in her blood.

He buried his face in her hair and inhaled. ''Oh, Tara you smell so good, feel so good,'' he said, running his hands over her bare skin as if to reassure himself that she was real and his.

''One more thing before I get too busy.'' He slid his fingertips over her breasts, then rubbed his thumbs over her nipples. She arched against him, thinking he'd already gotten busy.

''I've chosen who I want to head the charitable foundation,'' he said, lowering his lips to one of her already stiff nipples.

Tara struggled to concentrate. ''Who?''

''You.'' He lifted his head and looked at her with such a powerful combination of passion, trust and love that she could hardly breathe.

''Me?'' she squeaked.

''You. There's no one on this earth I trust more to

manage the foundation. There's no one I trust more with my life.''

Tara's heart squeezed tight. ''Oh, Nicholas, I don't know what to say.''

He dipped his mouth over hers for a lingering kiss. ''You don't have to say anything,'' he said, and his eyes glinted devilishly. ''Unless you want to moan or scream a little.''

By the time he finished with her, she'd done both.

Epilogue

Nicholas was so proud, he could have burst the buttons on his jacket. As his wife walked across the small wooden platform for her master's degree diploma, he gave a loud, distinctly unroyal whistle and clapped his hands.

Tara tossed a sideways glance in his direction, but she couldn't hide her joy. It shone in her eyes and the wide smile that stretched from ear to ear. Nicholas just thanked his lucky stars he could be a part of it all. He had never felt more complete than he had during the last ten weeks he and Tara had shared together while she finished her degree and he studied with a local physician specializing in gerontology.

Grant York, Tara's father, stood beside him in the back of the room and joined him as they applauded.

"She did this all on her own," Grant said with a mixture of pride and regret in his voice. "She sure didn't get any help from me."

"I don't know about that," Nicholas said. "She tells me her dad wrote the book on the power of determination."

Surprise glinted in Grant's eyes. "Really," he said, then nodded as if the notion pleased him. "I wouldn't have missed this for the world," Grant said. "I have to leave for Chicago right after the ceremony, but I'm glad she's finally getting her moment in the sun." He gave Nicholas an assessing glance. "You know she was hell-bent and determined not to marry you even after I received the photos," he said in a low voice.

Nicholas nodded, remembering how he'd sweated, wondering if Tara would ditch his royal butt at the altar. "I wasn't sure she would go through with it until I saw her walk down the aisle."

"Well, you have me to thank for it," Grant said.

Nicholas did a double take. He couldn't wait to hear this. "How is that, sir?"

"I spent four hours on the phone explaining to her how marriage was the only way to save her reputation. She wasn't having any of it until I asked her how those photos could affect you. That stopped her in her tracks."

Nicholas stared at Grant, then looked at Tara as she rejoined the other candidates for degrees. His heart turned inside out. He should be used to the sensation since it seemed Tara turned his head and heart on a regular basis. "She married me to protect my reputation," he muttered in amazement.

"She did," Grant said. "Like I said, you have me to thank for it, and you can thank me by keeping her barefoot and pregnant. I want grandchildren."

Nicholas met his father-in-law's cagey gaze. The man was just as pushy as Nicholas's mother. "You can rest assured that I'll expose Tara to the possibility of pregnancy at every opportunity, but there won't be any babies until we're ready," he said, even though the notion of a child had sneaked into Nicholas's brain a few times lately. He would have said he was the last man interested in any familial chains that bind, but damn if he didn't like the idea of Tara growing big with his baby.

The dean conferred the degrees to the small group of candidates, and Tara walked toward them.

"What do you mean when she's ready?" Grant asked.

"I mean Tara is going to be busy. She has accepted the position of Director of the Free Clinic Support Charity."

It was Grant's turn to give a double take. "Director?"

"Is there anyone else I could trust to do a better job?" Nicholas asked.

Grant hesitated a microsecond, then shook his head and smiled. "No one," he said, and opened his arms to Tara. "Congratulations, sweetheart. I couldn't be more proud."

Tara gave her father a big hug. "Thanks, Dad. It means so much that you could come."

Grant pulled back and Nicholas would almost swear he could see a tear in the tough tycoon's eye. "You know I believe you can do anything you want," Grant said in a gruff voice.

She smiled. "High praise coming from you."

"I mean it," her father said, rubbing her chin with his thumb. "And if you should decide you want children…"

Tara laughed, and the rich full sound filled up Nicholas's heart. "I'll let you know." She kissed her father on the cheek. "Thanks again for coming, Dad."

Grant gave a salute, then strode out of the room. His jet was waiting.

Still smiling, Tara turned to Nicholas and just looked at him, her eyes full of a dozen emotions.

He took her hand in his. "How does it feel?"

"Great," she said. "Kinda."

"Kinda?"

"A big part of the reason I was so determined to finish this degree was because I wanted to feel good enough for you. I'm happy and relieved that I finished, but I'm still just me."

"Just you," Nicholas said in disbelief, drawing her against him. "Silly woman, you have always been good enough. Don't ever forget that."

"That sounds like an order."

"It is," he said. "Now what does the graduate want to do?"

"Eat a quick bite and leave for Marceau," she said. "We're packed and ready to go. I want to see our new house."

He studied the faint blue circles beneath her eyes. He had noticed she'd seemed more tired during the last month and attributed it to her intense study schedule. It seemed she grabbed a nap at every opportunity. "Are you sure you don't want to go somewhere for a couple days of rest? You've earned it."

She shook her head, and her tassel bobbed. "I want to get to our house. The sooner, the better."

"As you wish, Your Highness," he said.

She swatted him. "I'm not sure I'll ever get used to the new title."

"Maybe if I start calling you Princess in bed," he said and tugged at the tassel on her mortarboard. "Speaking of which, this tassel gives me some ideas."

As promised, Tara and Nicholas ate a quick meal, then boarded a private jet for Marceau. Nicholas noticed she picked at her food, and as soon as the jet took off, Tara fell asleep. She slept the entire flight. He awakened her just as they prepared to land.

When she fell back asleep during the limo ride to their new house, he fought an undercurrent of concern. Her need for rest was natural, he told himself, but he couldn't help wondering if something else might be wrong. He searched his mind for symptoms she may have exhibited during the last few weeks.

Fatigue, poor appetite. He frowned, deciding to arrange for her to visit the palace doctor.

The limo pulled into the gated drive of the two-story stone villa his aide had chosen with the assistance of Maggie and Michelina.

Tara awakened and sheepishly covered a yawn. "I'm sorry," she murmured and looked outside the window. "We're here. It's beautiful."

Nicholas took her by the hand and led her to the front door where a housekeeper stood waiting. Just before they entered, he swooped her up in his arms to carry her into the house.

Tara gave a start of surprise.

"Since we married in a rush, we missed a few traditions."

"Like carrying the bride across the threshold," she said and met his gaze. "Are you trying to make me feel like a bride again?"

"I'm hoping I can talk you into doing something with that tassel. Second honeymoon," he said.

"I could have sworn you were antimarriage," she said.

"You changed my mind."

She bit her lip in a surprising show of nerves. "I hope so," she muttered.

Nicholas wondered where her doubts had come from. Despite her protests, he carried her to the master bedroom on the second floor. She looked around the room, nodding in approval at the blue and ivory décor. "Maggie and Michelina did a very nice job," Tara said. "But I want you to see another room."

Puzzled, he glanced at her and allowed her to slide to her feet. "What room?"

She inhaled and took his hand. "This way," she said, and walked with him down the hallway. They passed a bathroom and linen closet, then Tara pulled him into a freshly painted, but empty room. She pulled away from him.

"I need to tell you something, and I'm afraid," she said, biting her lip.

The fear in her eyes made his gut clench. "What is it? You can tell me anything."

Her expression full of uncertainty, she gave a nod that lacked conviction. "You know how I've been tired a lot lately?"

Nicholas's stomach turned, and he mentally clicked through a list of terminal diseases. "Have you been hiding something from me about your health?"

She wrung her hands together. "Kinda," she said and her eyes grew shiny with tears.

Alarm shot through him and he moved to take her in his arms. "Tara, what—"

She lifted her hand to keep him away. "This is difficult, so just let me finish. I know you didn't want to get married, but you did. I also know that even when you got married, you didn't plan to get so emotionally involved."

"But I did."

"Right. Well there's another thing I'm pretty sure you didn't plan."

"And that is?" he prompted over a hard knot in his throat.

She paused for a long moment, then met his gaze. "I'm pregnant," she said and her face crumpled. "That's why I brought you in here. This is going to be the nursery. I know you didn't really want to get married, and you probably didn't want to start a family for years, but—"

Relief coursed through him and he pulled her against him. "Why didn't you tell me?"

"I was afraid you'd be disappointed," she said, her voice cracking and breaking his heart. "A wife is enough baggage without adding another little person."

"Tara, how could you think that?"

She looked up and met his gaze. "I know what your goals are, and they don't include a baby."

He lifted his hand to her cheek, amazed at how she'd changed his point of view. "They didn't," he corrected. "Past tense. I didn't want to get married until I met you. You changed my mind. Don't you understand? I'm a better doctor by having you in my life. I'm a better man." He touched her still-flat abdomen with wonder and kissed her deeply. "I wonder if she'll have your smile."

"Who?"

"Our baby."

Tara searched his gaze as if she were afraid to hope. "I was hoping *he* would have your eyes," she said tentatively.

Nicholas grinned. "I was thinking *she* would have your determination."

"Or *he* might have your intelligence."

"Or *she* would have yours."

She looked at him with a mixture of surprise and faint exasperation. "I can't believe you've actually thought about having a baby with me."

"Believe it."

She swallowed. "What if we have a boy?"

"Then I will be proud as hell and love him," Nicholas said, then added slyly, "And we can try again."

Tara blinked. "Pardon me? Again?"

"And again. As many times as you're willing."

She laughed nervously. "Why do you want a girl?"

"Because I think you should be reproduced."

Her eyes softened. "That's funny. I thought the same thing about you. Every night during the last few weeks, I made a wish just before I fell asleep that you would be happy when I told you about the baby." She shook her head in wonder and her blue eyes filled with tears. "You made my wish come true."

Nicholas's chest felt tight as he took a deep breath. "Tara, I want to make all your wishes come true," he said. And she had every confidence he would succeed.

* * * * *

Silhouette Desire

presents

DYNASTIES: THE CONNELLYS

A brand-new miniseries about the Connellys of Chicago,
a wealthy, powerful American family tied by blood to the
royal family of the island kingdom of Altaria.
They're wealthy, powerful and rocked by
scandal, betrayal…and passion!

Look for a whole year of glamorous and
utterly romantic tales in 2002:

January: **TALL, DARK & ROYAL** by Leanne Banks

February: **MATERNALLY YOURS** by Kathie DeNosky

March: **THE SHEIKH TAKES A BRIDE** by Caroline Cross

April: **THE SEAL'S SURRENDER** by Maureen Child

May: **PLAIN JANE & DOCTOR DAD** by Kate Little

June: **AND THE WINNER GETS…MARRIED!** by Metsy Hingle

July: **THE ROYAL & THE RUNAWAY BRIDE** by Kathryn Jensen

August: **HIS E-MAIL ORDER WIFE** by Kristi Gold

September: **THE SECRET BABY BOND** by Cindy Gerard

October: **CINDERELLA'S CONVENIENT HUSBAND**
by Katherine Garbera

November: **EXPECTING…AND IN DANGER** by Eileen Wilks

December: **CHEROKEE MARRIAGE DARE**
by Sheri WhiteFeather

Silhouette®

Where love comes alive™